In the City
of the King

In the City of the King

William Pasnak

A Groundwood Book
Douglas & McIntyre
Vancouver/Toronto

Douglas & McIntyre Ltd.
1615 Venables Street
Vancouver, British Columbia

Canadian Cataloguing in Publication Data

Pasnak, William, 1949–
   In the city of the King

ISBN 0-88899-027-8

I. Title.

PS8581.A86I5 1984   jC813'.54   C84-098540-1
PZ7.P37In 1984

Cover art by Ian Wallace
Design by Maher & Murtagh
Printed and bound in Canada by D.W. Friesen & Sons Ltd.

To those who have endured for the sake of friendship.

1

In by the Back Door

There is a place on the borders of the highlands of Estria, a low hill. Looking back from it, you can see clear across the high plain to the mountains. Looking forward, you can see the land fall suddenly away to the rolling lowlands below. Beyond, in the far distance, there is the shifting and twinkling of the sea, and on its shore the spires and domes of Rakhbad, the City of the King.

One bright springtime day, a young girl sat on the brow of the hill singing a sweet and lonely song. She was small, slight and dark, dressed in a ragged jerkin and tights. As she sang, the wind ruffled her hair.

A man sat a little way off in the grass, a long thin man with a lean brown face folded and creased by the weather. His eyes were deep-set, a faded blue. Just now, they were fixed intently on the girl.

If I could see my true love come riding up the hill,
I'd slip away and wait for him, I know the spot quite well.

The only accompaniment to the girl's clear voice was the rushing of wind through grass. The girl did not look at the man, but stared at a patch of ground to one side of him, self-consciously beating time with one hand.

I'd slip away and wait for him, and never say a word.
For my heart has wings to fly to him, as swift as any bird.

When she finished, she ducked her head in a kind of a bow, and blushed.

"Well sung, Elena," the man applauded. "It's a very sweet piece that makes me think of the fine court ballads of Tadobal. Have you been working on it long?"

"Since we passed that water-carrier yesterday."

"Well, it is very good, and we may be able to use it in Ballafan. Just remember to look up and smile from time to time."

"I will," said Elena, standing up. "I do, usually. Where is Ballafan?"

"It's a small village some miles from here. I think tomorrow is market day, so we may have some luck."

"Is there an inn?"

"A stopping-house, as I recall, too small for us to play, and we haven't the silver to stay there."

"We'll have some after we play the market," said Elena with assurance.

"Maybe." Ariel got to his feet and picked up his pack. "I hope so. It's always a gamble, when you come fresh to a village or a country. What else have they heard and seen? How have the crops been, and the taxes? Have they been cheated recently? I came into a town once on the heels of a trickster who had been selling charms and feather dusters with the claim that you could fly with them strapped to your arms."

"What happened?" asked Elena, as she too struggled into the harness of her pack.

"I arrived as they were reviving some poor fellow under the town pump. Fortunately he had only jumped from a chicken coop. But the townspeople were rather hostile to strangers, and I didn't stay there long. Are you ready?"

8

"Wait. I have to tie this string."

Ariel gazed across the lands below. It had been years since he had come this way, through the back door of Estria, as it were, but the lines and folds of the hills stood out sharply in his memory. A little farther down, he remembered, there was a shepherd's cottage where he had once been given some cheese and a bit of bread. Beyond lay Ballafan, and then other towns and villages scattered across the lowlands, lush now with greening fields and orchards. And at the very edge of sight, their destination, Rakhbad. At the thought of it, Ariel frowned. As the royal city, Rakhbad should have been the safest city in all the realm, but beneath the glittering wealth and majesty, there lurked a darkness, a shadow.

On his last visit there, Ariel had sensed a dangerous seed that awaited the least inattention of the King to grow. What would they find this time? He had no way of knowing. It was over a year since any news at all from the court had reached him.

"Ready," said Elena then, and they set off down the slope.

They came to the shepherd's cottage about midday. The door swung idly in the wind; inside it was barren and cheerless, and smelled of mice. Elena saw the hearth was littered with rain-soaked ashes.

"Too bad," said Ariel. "I was hoping for a bit of a hand-out here. Well, never mind. We've still got a little food."

"Did they die?" asked Elena, gazing around the small, weed-grown yard.

"They might have," answered Ariel. "They were old enough when I was here before. Come round the side, we'll sit out of the wind for a bit."

With their backs against the stone wall of the cottage and their legs stretched out before them in the spring sunshine, they opened the food wallet and shared the last of their provisions: three dried apples and a tiny lump of goat's cheese.

"But I'm not very full," said Elena, when the last crumb had disappeared.

"Never mind," said Ariel. "I'll fill you up with pebbles." And he picked up a small stone from beside the wall and began to rub it. "Now, sit up straight, that's right, hands back like this, no like this, that's good, now here we go—there!" And before Elena knew what he was doing, he had pressed the rock against her stomach and seemingly rubbed it right inside, for his hand, which he held out for inspection, was completely empty.

Elena giggled. "Do that again," she said.

"Oh, still have some room inside, do you?" said Ariel, picking up another stone. "All right, now make sure you're not slouching, that's right, have to have room inside or the stone won't go in, lean back and there! You must be full by now!"

Elena giggled again. "More," she said. "One more."

Ariel put on a comic face and peered at her stomach. "Not full yet?" he said, marvelling. "I've known young girls to have ferocious appetites, but this is the most remarkable I've ever seen. Very well," he said, picking up a fist-sized stone, "I hope this will satisfy you. You'll have trouble walking with these stones inside you. Hard on the digestion, too. Now," he said as he rubbed the stone furiously, "this will take some pushing. Best brace yourself, put your arms out behind, that's the way, now, here we go—"

But just as he leaned over to push the stone home, Elena twisted around and seized his wrist. Grinning triumphantly, she said, "Show me. Show me the stone." Smiling in return, Ariel turned his hand over, empty. Still holding his wrist, Elena leaned over and drew forth from under his leg all three stones.

"I caught you," she said gleefully. "I caught you."

"Yes, you did," said Ariel. "But it took you three tries."

They came at last to Ballafan at nightfall, and they found their entrance to the village barred by a stout gate. A rough voice on the other side informed them it would not open till daylight. The best they could do was find some shelter under a hedge. Elena slept almost immediately, but Ariel lay awake pondering for some while: when last he came this way, Ballafan had no gate at all.

2

The Offer of a Fool

Ballafan was a good-sized village with a prosperous market. When Ariel and Elena walked into the square at the first light of dawn, they found people setting up stalls and laying out wares. There were rope makers and cobblers and old women with baskets, but Elena's hunger-sharpened eyes skipped over these, and sought out the stalls with cheese and fruit and bread.

"Where shall we set up?" she asked.

"Down there at the foot of the church steps," Ariel replied. "They give a little bit of height if we need it, and it will keep one side open. I don't like to be surrounded entirely."

It took them only a moment to spread out the beautiful sky-blue cloth on which they worked, and a moment more to take out the gleaming red and yellow balls painted with silver stars. Choosing three of them, Ariel stepped onto the middle of the cloth and stood for a moment with bowed head, absolutely still. Then "Hey—UP!" he cried, and suddenly the balls were in the air. As he whirled them about in a smooth and flowing circle, Elena stood close by in the cool morning air with more, ready to toss them to him, one by one.

"I'm slow this morning," said Ariel. "That hedge was damp last night."

"Mousy, too," said Elena. Her dreams had been criss-crossed by the scuttling of tiny feet.

In a moment more, Ariel said, "All right. Now." And Elena

tossed another ball into his hands. It was a moment that always made her tingle, for a slight hesitation or miscalculation on her part would ruin the show. They had practised in private, of course, and she had seen what a disaster a badly thrown ball could be, but in performance Ariel never seemed to worry. He trusted her completely.

"Another," said Ariel. "And another. And another." Now he was juggling seven balls. An audience gathered around them. After a moment more, Ariel flipped the balls back to Elena, who deftly caught them and placed them at the edge of the cloth. When all the balls were down, they started doing flips and vaults and springs. Elena was part of the act, which was arranged so that Ariel didn't look quite as good as he was, and Elena looked a good deal better than she was.

"That's showmanship," Ariel had told her. "People will want to watch you more anyway, because you're a girl and young besides."

The crowd of Ballafan was a good one, and enjoyed the show immensely. Even before the springs and jumps had ended, they began to toss pieces of money onto the cloth. Then for a change of pace, Elena sang her song, and drew a good response, too. Indeed, Elena thought it was more than she deserved, for she had lost her place at one point and left out an entire verse. The finale was Ariel juggling again, but this time standing on his head. During this, Elena made her way through the laughing and cheering crowd, smiling graciously and holding out a cap for money. Ariel had taught her that, too.

"You needn't be ashamed," he had told her. "We give a good show, and we must have bread to eat. But remember to smile, no matter what they do. Their hearts are more important than their money."

When Ariel finished the turn and the crowd began to drift away, he gathered up some of the money from the cloth, thrust it into Elena's hand and said, "Food." She needed no urging, for her own stomach was bitterly complaining. She hurried off towards the food stalls she had noticed earlier.

When she returned, laden with a couple of round loaves (one already half-eaten) and a good-sized cheese, she saw that one tall fellow from the crowd had lingered behind. He was dressed in the well-floured cap and apron of a miller, but his innocent stare and gap-toothed grin suggested that he might not have all his wits about him. He rocked on his heels and grinned at Ariel, who sat cross-legged on the church steps.

"Here," said Elena, giving Ariel a loaf and the cheese. "They haven't got much fruit here."

"Any food at all is a blessing," said Ariel, taking them from her. "I'm famished."

"That's a pretty cloth," the stranger suddenly blurted.

"Ay," replied Ariel mildly, looking at the man, "so it is."

The stranger grinned and chuckled to himself for no apparent reason. "Doesn't come from round here," he said.

"No," said Ariel. "It's Broden cloth."

"Ah," said the stranger, nodding and rocking all the while, "then you'll be a traveller."

Ariel looked at the man for a moment, and then said, "I follow the wind and the sun."

The man laughed foolishly and said, "Have you been across the ocean?"

"I have seen the other shore," said Ariel, watching him steadily all the while.

"Few return from such a journey," said the man, rocking a little faster. The conversation seemed to excite him, though Elena couldn't tell why.

"Some do and never tell," said Ariel.

"That's best, when there's wolves about." Then the stranger stopped rocking, and with a wide-eyed and serious stare, said simply, "Good-bye," turned, and left. Ariel watched him go,

14

and then resumed counting the money, chewing hungrily as he did so.

"Poor man," said Elena. "He must be simple. I hope he has someone to look after him." Ariel glanced at her, but said nothing. "Ariel," she went on, picking at a bur in her hair, "Will we have to sleep in the fields again tonight? Couldn't we bribe the guards to let us stay in town, maybe in a corner of the church?"

"We would need all this and more to bribe any self-respecting guard," said Ariel, tying the money in a cloth and putting it in a purse. "But all the same, you get your wish. We will be sleeping inside tonight."

"Where?" asked Elena.

"As guests of our friend the miller."

"You mean that simpleton?"

"I mean the man that stayed and spoke to us after the show," said Ariel. "Unless I'm very much mistaken, he's no fool. Although he may very well appear so to the unwary," he added, looking at Elena.

"How do you know we can stay with him?" she demanded, ignoring the pointed reference.

"Well, he asked us to, more or less."

"I didn't hear him ask us."

"You weren't meant to. He was speaking a kind of secret tongue, used by—Good morning, Constable!" said Ariel suddenly. "A fine day to you, sir."

Standing over them was a large, red-faced man with tiny eyes and a big belly. He wore no uniform, but from his wrist dangled a large club, and he looked hot, out of breath and irritated.

"Where are you from," he demanded roughly.

"We come from Mulabruk, across the high plains," said Ariel.

"Bound for where?"

"We are journeying to Rakhbad, to the court of the King."

"Oh, the court, is it?" scoffed the constable. "Royalty, I suppose you are! The likes of you at the court of the King! Well, you can stay for the market, but if I find you here after sunset, I'll thrash the hides off you! Understand?" And he huffed away without waiting for an answer.

"What were you saying," asked Elena when he was gone, "about a secret language?"

"Not here," said Ariel in a low voice. "I'll tell you when we're someplace safer."

3

Words in the Dark

It was almost sunset when they neared the mill, which stood alone on a stream beyond the gate of the village. Ariel had been at great pains to make sure no one saw them going there. They had left Ballafan in the other direction and then circled around through the fields.

"Is it because of the constable?" asked Elena, as they lay beneath some bushes, a stone's throw from the mill. Their way was blocked by two old wives who had stopped to gossip in the road and were busy trading symptoms.

"Not only him," said Ariel. "There's other eyes we should avoid as well."

"Whose?"

"I don't know," said Ariel.

When they arrived at the mill at last, it seemed deserted. The wheel was still, the door and shutters closed, and there was no sound or sign of movement. But when they came to the door, it opened before they could knock, and the miller beckoned them in.

He shut the door behind them, and beckoning again, led them across the dusty stone floor to a ladder. He whispered, "I must go out. Go up there and stay still till I return."

The ladder led to a loft that contained the large wooden gears of the mill wheel. Sacks of flour were piled beside a square loft door and the room was dusty and very dim. The only light crept in around the edges of the door. As they made themselves comfortable on the sacks, Ariel and Elena heard the door below close and, peering through a crack in the wall, they watched the miller hasten towards the village with a sack thrown over his shoulder. It suddenly seemed very quiet in the gathering dark of the loft.

For a long time, Ariel and Elena stared at each other. They could see little more than the gleam of each others' eyes, and the only sound they could hear was the murmur of the brook outside. Finally Ariel spoke.

"Well," he said softly, "is it better than a damp hedgerow of mice and burdock?"

"Ariel," said Elena, "what is this all about? Who is that man? And why must we be so secret here? And where did he go off to now, with a sack across his back?"

"To answer your last question first," said Ariel, "I don't know where he's gone. As to who he is, he is a miller, called Sarafin, I think, or so I gather from the market gossip I heard today. And as for why we must be so secret, it is because he is a miller and something other than a miller, too."

"What, then?" asked Elena, her eyes wide in the dark. She could not imagine him being anything other than a miller, unless it were a lunatic. She could still see clearly his foolish grin and innocent stare.

"He is," said Ariel in a low voice, "or should be, from all appearances, a Fellow of the Brotherhood of the Silent Heart."

"You mean a sorcerer?"

"No," said Ariel. "He is not a sorcerer. He is member of the Brotherhood, both a lesser and a greater thing than a sorcerer. Whatever that is," he added. "I have never met a real one."

"But does he work magic? Can he fly?"

"Perhaps he can," said Ariel. "I don't know. The Brothers

don't do anything but live their lives and look within them-selves for whatever truth they can find there. And in each person that truth takes a different form. Some work miracles and some are gentle, honest men. But they always work in secret.''

Elena felt a chill run down her back. She had heard of secret societies and brotherhoods before. There were always rumours around markets about covens and secret bands of sorcerers, which always met with grisly ceremony in the dead of night to work all kinds of mischief. But in all her travels, Elena had never seen tail or toe of a witch, sorcerer or secret brotherhood.

Until now.

"Ariel," she said in a hushed voice, "is it—safe, here?"

"No," said Ariel. "It's not. Sarafin we can trust with our lives. But in coming here, that's likely what we have done— put our lives in his hands. There's danger about, though I don't yet know what kind."

"Then why are we here? Why are we meddling with this Brotherhood, and how do you know about them?"

Ariel turned and for a long moment peered through the crack. At last he turned to her and said in a low voice, "Elena, I told you the Brotherhood always works in secret. They live their lives and try, in the midst of their extraordinary schooling, to seem like ordinary men. For the past twenty years *I* have been a member of the Brotherhood. I never told you before, because the Brotherhood is secret and there are some places where even to know of its existence means death. But I tell you now because I think there is need. It is not an easy burden I lay upon you, for if you should ever let it slip to the wrong person it would be the end of you, and probably others, too. But from what the miller said this morning, something is afoot, and I think it best you know."

"But what did he say?" asked Elena. "I only heard him talk about travelling."

"Yes, he did talk about travelling, but it was a code, a kind of secret language. That he should use it at all, and from the forms he used, it seems there is great danger here, and great urgency, too."

"Then how did—"

"Hush!" said Ariel. "Somebody is coming."

Sure enough, on the road below someone was approaching the mill. To Elena's ears, straining in the sudden stillness, it sounded as though whoever it was came slowly, perhaps with a limp.

"Maybe it's him," she whispered. "The miller."

Ariel did not reply; he put his finger to his lips and shook his head. The steps had reached the mill now, and for a brief instant Elena thought they might pass by, but the slow dragging sound stopped. There was a long pause. Then came a muffled knock. Elena stirred, but Ariel reached out and put his hand over hers where it lay on the sacking. In a moment the knocking came again, and then, to Elena's horror, the latch clicked and the door creaked open and closed again.

Elena listened to the slow dragging step cross the floor of the dark room below. In the pitch black of the loft, she was grateful for the touch of Ariel's warm hand on hers. Suddenly as they sat holding their breaths in the darkness, light bloomed in the square ladderway.

Elena stared at the wavering light. Her hands were wet and her stomach felt tight and cold. *What can they want?* she thought. *Are they looking for us?* And she thought again of Ariel's words: In some places, even to know of the existence of the Brotherhood means death.

The light grew much brighter. The candle must have been at the foot of the ladder. There was a brief shuffling sound, and then Elena felt the vibration of a heavy foot on the first rung.

A thousand thoughts flew through her head as she stared at

the mounting brightness in the ladderway. The loft was plain and open, and offered no place to hide. How could they move now without being heard? In a moment they would be in full sight of whoever was climbing the ladder. Elena glanced at Ariel; his face was impassive.

The candle and the hand that held it were already visible when suddenly the door below flew open with a bang, and a voice shouted, "Hey! Who's that climbing up there?"

"I's me," slurred the voice from the ladder. "Basket. Gonna sleep inna lof'."

"And burn the place to the ground. No you aren't," replied the first voice. "This is no inn for drunken layabouts. Come down and get out."

Although Basket grumbled and argued a great deal, he did climb back down the ladder, and very soon after was thrust out into the night. As he stumbled away, protesting bitterly, there was a scramble up the ladder, and the loft was flooded with light.

"I'm sorry," said Sarafin, gazing down at them where they sat, blinking, on the sacks. "I hope he didn't disturb you."

4

The Meeting in the Hidden Chamber

Elena followed Ariel and Sarafin across the loft to a little door hidden in the wall behind the mill gears. The miller no longer seemed a simpleton; his face was shining as he turned to them.

"I would have sent you in here directly if I had known old Basket was about. Mind your heads, and close the door behind you." And he disappeared through the doorway.

Elena found herself in a narrow, low passage. Ariel and Sarafin were forced to stoop almost double. It appeared not to be a real passage but rather an extra space in the building between a wall and the roof. It didn't seem to lead anywhere in particular. Elena passed unfinished timbers, stone and dust before she emerged at the other end, in a room little bigger than their performing cloth, with a sloping ceiling that on one side was no higher than Elena herself.

"We are safe here," said Sarafin, setting down the light and pulling cushions from a corner. "A place unknown to anyone hereabouts. You may stay here as long as you wish."

Elena looked about the small, tidy space. Some cushions, a low shelf, a small brazier and teapot were its only furnishings. From outside came the gentle wash and gurgle of the mill stream, like someone talking quietly in another room.

"Now, welcome, Brother, fellow traveller," said Sarafin as he embraced Ariel.

"Peace be with *you*, traveller," said Ariel as they separated. "I am Ariel, and this is Elena."

"And I am Sarafin. Greetings." The miller bent down to embrace Elena. All in an instant she felt his breath, rough cloth, a firm hug. Before she could respond, he had straightened up again.

"Please sit down," he said, "and tell me if there is anything you need."

"Only talk for now," said Ariel, sinking onto a cushion. "We have much to catch up on."

"Good!" said Sarafin. "Talk is what I crave, too. Well, tell me, first, where did you come from?"

"Across the highlands from Alta-Kep. Before that Washoe, Sumner, Mirza and the South Shores."

"A long way! Then I must give *you* the news, though I live so far from anywhere but here."

"Ay, what news?" demanded Ariel. "Is all well with the Brothers?"

"I believe the Brotherhood is well," replied Sarafin. "As well as may be. But we seem to have lost the King."

"Lost the King?" said Elena. "You mean the King is dead?"

Sarafin looked at her in surprise. "Why no, little sister, King Akheem reigns still. I mean *we* have lost him. The Brotherhood has lost him from the web."

"Elena is but newly come to the order," said Ariel. "I have not told her of the web."

"Indeed?" said Sarafin, and glanced keenly first at Elena and then at Ariel. Elena saw the unspoken question pass between them. "No," said Ariel, "she is safe and true, I can vouch for that. But only tonight have I told her of the Brotherhood. I felt there was need," he added, "for her and for us."

Sarafin looked at Elena for a moment. "Very well," he said, "if you will answer for her, I am glad to have her for a sister. And you are right—there *is* need. Well, Elena, the Brotherhood is small, but widely spread, I think, though no one seems to know how many Brothers there actually are. Some have different ways of counting Brothers than others, for one thing. But each one of us bears a responsibility for the world. As much of the world as we can see. Even the poorest and most ragged brother receives fresh air and sunlight, and countless other gifts we can never repay. Well, our gift in return, in this land anyway, is to see that the King rules well."

"Rules well?" said Elena. "What do you mean?"

"Ruling is an art," replied Sarafin. "Some kings rule better than others. Some kings are thoughtful of their people, while others are fitful and heedless. Our duty is to help each king rule as well as he is able."

"How?"

"By understanding, by concentration and by the web. We have ways of knowing and feeling things, and ways of sending information that are . . . better than the general way. And so we serve the King the way a web serves a spider, each strand sending its own vibration to the centre."

"Then you are spies," said Elena in surprise.

"Spies? No. Say counsellors, rather. Or guardians. Rarely does a king even know of our existence. You see, it is to our advantage to remain unknown, and let the King suppose that he has discovered for himself what is shown."

"But why?" demanded Elena. "Why not tell him straight out?"

"For a number of reasons," replied the miller. "Kings have human weaknesses. If our presence were known, it would be a natural temptation to misuse the web for selfish ends. Although this could not really be, the attempt would hamper us terribly. Another reason is effectiveness. What you tell a person is never heard as well as what he tells himself."

"Still another reason is safety," said Ariel. "The good

citizens of Estria are not free from superstition. If the folk of Ballafan, for instance, suspected we were meeting in a hidden room in the dead of night, not one stone of this mill would be left standing by the morning.''

Elena looked at the grave men before her. She knew what Ariel said was true. She had seen unreasoning fear in villages before.

"But what about the King?" said Ariel. "You said—"

"That we have lost the King," Sarafin affirmed. "Perhaps four months ago . . . something . . . began to interfere. Since then Akheem has become quite heedless, and the country has begun to suffer.''

Ariel looked at Elena, saw she did not understand, and said, "Do you recall the rope-walkers of the South Shores?"

"Yes," said Elena.

"They worked with a safety net, a small one held by three friends who followed below. Our web is a little like that. The King wanders where his fancy takes him, and we must follow, keeping him centred on the net.''

"But not a net in space," continued the miller. "A net in the mind. We must know where the mind of the King lies and have people about who can touch upon it. The last king, King Arben, for example, was a great huntsman, you know. Well, he ruled well for thirty years, partly because of the unobtrusive presence of his dog-keeper.''

"Who was a Brother?" asked Elena.

"Yes," said the miller. "But now, somehow, we have lost touch with King Akheem. His mind has changed. But I fear this is not a random shift. Some presence has intervened.'' Sarafin paused and looked first at Ariel and then at Elena. "If we cannot find a solution, it will be a disaster for the land of Estria.''

Elena stared into the shadows beyond the two men. She thought of all the stories she had heard on the road about cruel kings and countries ruined by harsh taxes, famine and senseless wars. She had never considered that such things could happen in her homeland.

At last Ariel spoke. "What has been done, then?"

"Do you know Barkat the perfume maker?" asked Sarafin. Ariel nodded. "He travels all about," said Sarafin to Elena, "gathering flowers and such for his trade. He was here a month ago with a load of highland lily, heading down to Rakhbad. We agreed then that he should try to see the King, and send out word of what he found."

Ariel said, "And there has been no word from him since?"

Sarafin shook his head. "None to Ballafan," he said. "Although silence does not in itself alarm me. But I am uneasy about him—in dreams I have seen him very weak and ill."

Ariel sat for a long time, pondering silently. At last he said, "Do you know Faradou?"

"A tall man? Red hair? I believe he moved from Rakhbad."

"Mm. Too bad. Washay?"

"A Brother?"

"Yes . . ."

As they passed down a seemingly endless list of names, Elena felt sleep stealing over her. The soft voices of Ariel and Sarafin lulled her now into a drowsy stupor. Without quite realizing it, she rolled off her cushion, gathered her cloak about her, and fell into a deep sleep.

Hours later she suddenly found herself wide awake, staring through the darkness, trying to remember where she was. For a moment, she could make no sense out of what she could see, and then memory and understanding flooded her at the same time. Before her sat Sarafin and Ariel, still as death, facing each other, their eyes closed.

Perhaps it was the trick of some stray moonbeam, but the air between them seemed to shimmer with a faint blue light.

5

Two Strangers and a Sack

Elena woke to the liquid sound of pigeons cooing in the rafters and the miniature feathered thunder of their wings. Looking up, she saw a small square window above her, just under the peak of the roof. A small patch of intense blue sky told her the day would be fine and warm; a good day for travelling.

"Good morning," came Ariel's voice from behind her. "Did you sleep well?"

"Like a bear," said Elena. Rolling over, she found herself face to upside-down face with Ariel, who was bent over backward, so that his head was behind his knees and his hands upon the floor. "And you?" asked Elena.

Ariel grinned, a sudden flash of teeth where his forehead should have been. "I slept more like a cat. When Sarafin and I were done, the sun was rising."

"I fell asleep," said Elena ruefully.

"You didn't miss much," said Ariel. "He told me how things have changed in Estria." Slowly he raised his legs into the air, so that he was standing on his hands. "There are lots of new rules. And taxes. And disorder. That sack we saw him with last night was some grain for a widow, so she could pay one of the taxes."

"Where is he now?"

"Gone down to start the mill, I think," said Ariel, righting himself and standing up. "He said we would be safer here with the sound of the mill to cover our voices." Even as he spoke, there came a heavy creaking and then a steady, deep rumbling that gently shook the floor.

"Aren't we going out today?" Elena had to raise her voice against the grumble of the millstones.

Ariel shook his head. "It's safer not."

"Safer for him?"

"It's better if strangers aren't seen about the mill too much."

Elena nodded, but she was disappointed. She was not used to being inside and had been looking forward to the warm sunshine on her back. *Why can't it be raining today?* she thought as she watched a pigeon swoop out the high window into the bright air beyond. But the sky, the small part she could see, remained obstinately cloudless.

The sound of the mill made more talk difficult. Ariel finished his exercises, curled up in a corner and went to sleep, leaving Elena to amuse herself as best she could. After a breakfast of oatcakes and jam that she found by one wall, she decided to explore as much of the hidden attic as she could.

She went down the passageway, but it was much as Elena had seen it the night before. At the far end, by the door, she found some tools, an old sack, a cracked mill gear. Any stranger looking in would think that this was all the doorway led to. Elena was about to turn back when she made out, in faint letters, on the inside of the door, the word ONE.

That's curious, she thought. *I wonder why that's there.*

At the other end of the corridor she systematically took stock of the room itself. She had half hoped there would be another secret passage leading to yet another secret room, but in this she was disappointed. Her thorough examination yielded only the cushions and blankets, the tea brazier, a small leather writing case, some candles, a water jar, a bag of dried figs. She also found more writing. In one corner, low down on the wall, she found a circle with a dot in the middle. Underneath was written, NOT ONE.

Maybe it's a riddle, she thought as she puzzled over the inscription.

When her search revealed no more, she pulled a bench over and, stretching up, managed to swing onto a beam by the window. As she did this, there was an explosion of wings, and three pigeons shot away into the sunlight.

"Sorry," said Elena. "I want to see out."

Flattened along the beam, she had a fair view out the window. From the right, a road came climbing out of town, passed just below her and curled away to the left around the corner of the mill. Beyond the road was the green edge of a field.

"Well, at least I can watch others on the road, if I can't be there myself," she said as she settled her chin on her hands.

But she found herself watching the pigeons more than the road. There was no market in Ballafan today, and very few people passed by. Once in a long while someone came trudging up the hill from town carrying a sack or a basket. Elena watched them disappear into the mill below her, and in a short while reappear to go trudging back down the hill, their grain transformed to puffing flour.

"No wonder Sarafin was so glad to see us," she thought. "Nothing ever happens here."

But towards midday she was startled by a sudden silence. The mill wheels had stopped. They had been so steady that they had become a sound forgotten. Now, in the ringing silence, Elena felt light and free, and heard once again the sounds of the birds on the roof.

Presently she heard a movement below her, and looking around, saw Sarafin come into the room. When he noticed her on her perch, he smiled and said, "Good. You can be the lookout."

"What should I look out for?" she asked.

"I don't know," replied Sarafin. "But I have to go into town for a little while, and you can watch the road from there to see who comes and goes. Unless," he added, with a glance at the slumbering Ariel, "you would rather sleep."

"No," said Elena. "I'll watch."

"Good! I'll be back soon." And he left the room, humming to himself. A moment later, Elena heard him pull the mill door to. Then he came into view, striding briskly down the road to town.

So I'm a watchman, thought Elena, as she gazed out the window at the now empty road. *Well, there's precious little to watch from here. There don't seem to be any people around at all.*

Perhaps an hour had dragged by when the clip-clop of a horse and the jingle of harness came faintly to her ear. As the sound grew louder, Elena realized that it was an unusual one for Ballafan. At the market the day before, she had noticed that the people mostly went about on foot, or on donkeys. But this was definitely the brisk trot of a horse, coming up through town.

I wonder who it could be, thought Elena. The jingling got louder and louder until, as Elena watched, a horse, pulling an open cart with two men riding in it, came into view, toiling up the hill towards her.

The horse looked as though he might once have been a fine stallion, but now he was lathered and dusty, and ready to drop. The two men were strange, in a way Elena found difficult to pin down. They were not farmers, nor did they seem to be townspeople. Wrapped in dirty cloaks, their faces grim and haggard, they kept glancing around at the road behind them.

As the cart came up to the mill, the driver reined in and stopped just below Elena. She could only see the tops of the men's heads, but she could easily hear what they said.

"What are you stopping here for, dolt? Do you want to get us killed? Drive on!"

"This is the place he said," replied the other. "We promised."

"Promised!" spat the first voice. "You're an idiot. I should have thrown that sack in the sea."

The driver did not reply. He got down from the cart and knocked on the mill door. Elena held her breath.

After a moment, the man on the cart called in a hissing whisper, "There's no one there. Come on. Hurry!"

"But the sack," said the other. "We—"

"Blast the sack!" exclaimed the first. "If it weren't for that wretch, we wouldn't be in this fix." And grabbing a sack from the back of the cart, he flung it into the ditch on the far side of the road. "There!" he said with bitterness as he seized the reins and brought the exhausted horse to life again. "May it do him as much good there as he ever did to us!"

The rumble of the cart drowned out any further words. The other man scrambled onto the back of the cart as it swept out of sight around the corner.

"Well," Elena said at last, "Sarafin certainly knows when to set a watch!"

6

A Bracelet and Broken Words

Elena was burning to tell Sarafin of the two strange men and the sack and the whispered conversation. But for all her eagerness, one delay after another kept her from seeing him.

Before Sarafin returned, the constable from the market appeared on the road. "A sheriff," murmured Ariel, who had awakened and now was watching, too. "They call such a sheriff, hereabouts, I found out yesterday. With the new rules from Rakhbad, he is more like a tyrant."

The burly, red-faced figure stumped up the hill towards them. Finding the mill shut and apparently deserted, he impatiently paced up and down in the road. It seemed to Elena that at any moment he must see the sack lying in the ditch, in plain sight from where she was, and she watched with her heart in her mouth.

"What do you suppose he wants?" whispered Elena.

"Don't know," said Ariel. "Not us, I don't think."

The sheriff was still waiting when Elena saw the miller climb the hill. She thought she noticed a cloud pass across his face when he caught sight of the sheriff, but he called out cheerfully, "Hello, Sheriff! Need a loaf's worth?"

"I've come on the King's business," the sheriff growled. "Where have you been?"

"The King's business?" said Sarafin in amazement. "No! Does the King know about me?"

Elena, listening in the loft, was astonished to hear once again the voice of the half-witted miller of Ballafan. "He's changed!" she hissed to Ariel.

"Mm," he said and listened more intently.

"—civil tongue in your head," the sheriff was saying. "I want to ask you some questions about that cart."

"What cart?"

"Don't play the innocent with me. That cart with two strangers and a lathered nag that came up the highroad this afternoon."

"Strangers!" said Sarafin. "Are they stopping at the inn?"

"No, they can't stop anywhere. They're exiles. Headed for the border. But I want to know what they were doing up here by your mill."

"Well," said Sarafin, so slowly that Elena almost burst out laughing, "they has to go past it if they're heading for the border, don't they? Unless they was going the Tadderbury road, then they'd be way out of their way. They should go back down the village and across by Rastin's pasture."

"They stopped up here," said the sheriff shortly. "Tom Rapperty seen 'em."

"Did he?" replied Sarafin. "Well, you should ask him, then. I was down at the other end of town talking to Missus Covey about this sore arm I got, been twitching me since lambing time. But maybe," he added reflectively, "it was the hill tired their horse out. Did Tom say they was visitin'?"

"That old fool can't see more than the church steeple on a clear day," said the sheriff, "but he says he heard them stop up here for a few minutes. If you find that pair around here, you let them right alone. They're exiles, see? Don't speak to them or help them, or it's the same for you or worse!" And with that he left, swaggering down the dusty road to town.

"Exiles!" said Elena excitedly when he was gone. "They

were exiles, fleeing for their lives! What do you suppose they did?''

Ariel smiled wryly. "They may not have done anything,'' he said. "To be exiled merely means that someone in power is displeased with you. Perhaps the sack will tell us more.''

"Yes,'' said Elena, "I've got to tell Sarafin about the sack. But what if someone else finds it? Oh, I wish he'd hurry and come up!''

But just then they heard a halloo from outside and a voice calling for "Three sacks worth, please, miller.''

"Bother it,'' muttered Elena as the mill started up again. "Now he'll never get up here.''

Indeed, it was almost dark when the door was shut behind "three sacks worth'' and Sarafin came striding into the room, almost as excited and impatient as Elena. "What did you see?'' he demanded. "Anything? Tell me!''

When she had finished her tale of the strangers and the sack and the whispered conversation, Sarafin did not rush down to find the sack, but stood instead deep in thought. "What do you think?'' he said at last, looking at Ariel. "Is it safe?''

"Safe, but not too safe,'' Ariel replied. "I think the sheriff is all right, but the sack may be watched by others. Is there a quiet way out of here?''

Sarafin nodded. "A small door at the back that opens into bushes.''

"Then I'll go and see,'' said Ariel. "It might be easier for me.''

"Why?'' asked Elena.

"He doesn't live here,'' said Sarafin.

"That's right,'' said Ariel, and he put a look of innocent astonishment on his face. "Just a wandering tramp that found an old sack in the ditch. No harm in that, is there? Now, just show me the back door, Sarafin.''

As they went down together, Elena scrambled up to her

lookout and tried to follow Ariel's progress, but in the darkness she could only just make out the far side of the road. She was gazing intently at a patch of grey she thought was the sack when she heard a noise behind her, and turned to find Sarafin and Ariel back already. Ariel had the sack slung casually over one shoulder.

"I didn't even see you," she said, jumping down.

"I didn't mean to be seen," said Ariel. "Now let's find out what all this fuss is about."

Sitting cross-legged on the floor, he thrust his arm deep into the sack and drew forth a small package. He handed it to Sarafin. "That's all," he said.

Wordlessly, Sarafin turned the package over, examining it. It was a tattered bundle of bright red and gold cloth. Sarafin unrolled it, revealing two objects.

"A bracelet," said Elena, gazing at the circlet of silver.

"And a letter," said Sarafin. "Or part of one." He picked up a thin shaving of wood the size of a man's hand. One side was covered with fine writing. "Parts of it have broken away," said Sarafin. "The salutation and the signature. The part that is here reads, '—is my true friend and a capable fellow. He has requested me, my lord, to recommend him to you. I therefore ask you, my lord, that whatever he may request of you, you will agree to let him have. That through helping him, you will have put me under an obligation to you as your debtor.' And scrawled across the bottom, in another hand, are the words 'Farewell Brother.' "

Ariel broke the silence. "This message came to you, Sarafin. How do you read it?"

"It comes from Barkat, certainly. But I fear it bodes ill for him. The letter is an introduction, likely meant to gain an audience at court for him. Perhaps with the King, perhaps with some official. This," he said, fingering the cloth, "is the sleeve of some finery. Maybe he did indeed gain an audience, probably wearing a fortune on his back for the occasion. The bracelet too suggests that. But the sleeve is in tatters, the letter broken. This and the message 'Farewell Brother'—for it *is* his hand—say that his venture into court life ended in disaster.''

"And the messengers?'' said Ariel.

"The exiles? Perhaps the unfortunates who introduced him to the court. I fear that Barkat is in danger for his life if it is not already too late.''

"Yes,'' said Ariel. "I read the same. But the bracelet is more sinister than mere court finery. Look!''

Peering closely in the lamplight, Elena saw that the bracelet was wrought in the form of a snake with a crescent moon upon its forehead. Along its sides, imitating scales, were written the words AXOS ABBA SAMOXAS.

"What is this?'' said Sarafin.

"I saw such a bracelet once on a dead priest in Nysos,'' said Ariel. "The words mean 'Death Follows After,' and those who wear them are . . . evil. *They* are sorcerers, if you like, Elena. They do not believe in any life but this, they are blind to the immortal spirit, and so in fear and desperation they try to bend this life to their will. They are self-serving, hungry for power, and very, very dangerous.''

Ariel took the bracelet between forefinger and thumb, studied it for a moment, then carefully set it down on the stained and tattered sleeve.

"If such men have the ear of the King,'' said Ariel, "far more than Barkat's life is in danger. The kingdom itself may teeter upon the brink of ruin.''

7

Towards Rakhbad

The next evening, Ariel and Elena sat by a small fire in a grove of trees far from the town of Ballafan. They had travelled all day and part of the night to get there. Following the examination of the sack, Ariel, Elena and Sarafin had held a brief, urgent council, and decided that Ariel and Elena must make all speed for Rakhbad. Accordingly, and as they were fresh from a day of rest, they set out that night.

"Journey well," Sarafin had said as they were leaving. "I feel you are going to a labour that is most important and most deadly. I wish it were mine to share with you. Take care, little sister," he added, clasping Elena by the hand. "Be vigilant and sharp-eyed as you were this afternoon, and remember, if you need help, help lies within."

And Elena, turning from him at the door, was surprised to find that her eyes were stinging with tears.

Now, many hours and miles later, she and Ariel sprawled by their little fire and chewed on round, moist loaves the miller had given them. All about them was the stillness and shadow of night.

"Ariel," said Elena through a full mouth, "what will we do when we get there?"

"Nothing," said Ariel. "Visit. Perform."

Elena considered this for a moment. "Then why are we making such a rush to get there?"

Ariel grinned. "What I mean is, I don't know what we will do, and I won't know until I have talked to a few old friends there and learned more about this mystery. Until then, like good spies, we will do nothing except live our ordinary lives."

"Do you think we can save Barkat?"

Ariel frowned. "It may be so. If he was flung in a dungeon and forgotten, we may be able to arrange his release or his escape. But we don't know what his 'crime' was. He may already be dead."

"How will you find out?"

"My friends will know. But saving Barkat is not our first task. Or it may be our first, but it is not our most important. Far more important than Barkat's life are the heart and mind of the King." Ariel was interrupted by a sudden halloo from the direction of the road.

"Who's there?" shouted a voice.

"A poor juggler," Ariel called in reply. "Who seeks to know?"

"Soldiers of the King. Stay where you are!"

Ariel and Elena exchanged glances but said nothing as they listened to the approach of heavy booted footsteps through the brush.

In a moment, a large figure clad in the brass and leather of a soldier strode into the circle of firelight and said, "Hadrat, sergeant of the King's Patrol. State your name and business."

"Hullo, Hadrat," said Ariel affably. "I haven't seen you since the old days in Westban. What are you beating about up here for?"

"What—Ariel!" said Hadrat. "I might have thought it was you, when you said a juggler. I haven't seen you in a dozen years! How are you?"

"Sound and whole, as you see me," said Ariel. "And it seems you are the same, though I think you've grown since we parted."

Hadrat laughed enormously and slapped his belly, which was solid and well filled out. "I guess I have, hey? Peacetime is no good for a soldier. But tell me, Ariel, who is this young maid? Not your daughter, is she?"

"This is Elena," said Ariel with a courteous bow. "The leading lady of our little band. I travel with her and learn what I can."

"Oh, indeed," said Hadrat. "Well, I'm honoured to meet you, Miss Elena. But I wager the teaching and learning mostly go the other way. I knew Ariel years ago, and he knew more then than a basketful of magistrates, though where he learned it all I couldn't say. I only ever saw him in the kitchen juggling potatoes."

"Why don't you join us," said Ariel. "We've little to offer but some bread and a warm fire, but you're welcome to what we have."

"That I cannot do," said Hadrat. "I'm under strict orders not to stop until we reach the border."

"Oh?" said Ariel. "Something up? We just came down that way a few days ago. It seemed quiet enough."

Hadrat gave a grimace of distaste. "No, it's nothing to do with the border. It's these poor fool exiles we're chasing after. You didn't see them, did you?"

"Perhaps," said Ariel. "Are you supposed to catch them?"

"Not unless they are fools enough to stay in Estria."

"We saw them yesterday, heading out from Ballafan at a fast trot."

"Good!" said Hadrat. "For I'll tell you true, I don't want to catch them. Some exiles it would give me great pleasure to find hiding in a cowshed, but not these ones."

Ariel cocked his head at the sergeant. "You don't think them guilty?"

"Well, they might be, at that," said Hadrat grudgingly. "I've seen enough of people in my life to know they're as contrary and unpredictable as winter weather in Haverbord. But to my mind,'' and he glanced about at the night and dropped his voice, ''it's far more likely to be the work of that black viper's brood that's made its nest in the Palace these past months.''

''Oh?'' said Ariel. ''Priests, would that be?''

''Priests!'' spat Hadrat. ''Cold black devils and trouble-makers! I see you've heard of them.''

''Almost nothing. We've just returned from abroad.''

''Well, you'll hear more if you're travelling down country. I wouldn't say this to just anyone, Ariel, but between you and me, since they moved in, it's been worth your life to come to court, what with accusations, and 'plots' uncovered, and 'strange accidents.' And it's got now so people don't come to court unless they're asked, and the King isn't asking.''

''Why doesn't someone throw them out?'' asked Ariel.

''Don't think it hasn't been tried! But those as tried it ended up like these two, exiled, or worse. I tell you, these Priests have got some power, and it isn't just from having the ear of the King.''

''I see,'' said Ariel.

''But I can't stop here all night chattering. As I say, if you're bound down country, you'll hear more about it soon enough. More than you care to! Ariel, Elena, if you ever need a friend in the King's Patrol, remember to ask for Hadrat.''

And then, with a shout to stir his men, he was gone, crashing through the bushes to the road.

8

The Well of Ismay

As they travelled on towards Rakhbad the next day, Elena felt they were walking into a completely different world. The country, the road, the people, even the air seemed to have changed overnight. As they descended into the broad coastal plain, the fields changed and opened, trees were replaced by low hedges, and the road widened into a busy thoroughfare. It was warmer, too. On the high plain, it had been the beginning of spring. Now, in the warm thick air of the lowlands, it seemed like summer, and Elena was glad to stow her cloak away in her pack.

Since Ariel did not seem inclined to talk, Elena hummed to herself, running through her repertoire of ballads. Some had been taught to her by Ariel, some she had picked up from listening to others and some she had composed herself. She was surprised by how many she knew.

"Ariel," she said, "I'm a balladeer. I know more than two score of songs."

Ariel roused himself from his thoughts to gaze at her a moment.

"I know 'Ismay's Sorrow,' 'The White Swan,' 'Two Red Shoes to Dance In' . . . ." She counted them off on her fingers.

But Ariel's thoughts were elsewhere, and when she finished he merely said, "Good. Very good," and fell back into his reverie. Only much later did he break the silence to say, "Ismay was real, you know. We shall come to her well soon."

"Her well?" said Elena. "What well?"

"The well referred to in the song: 'the gentle water flowing-o.' When Ismay met her brother Polyno coming home from the battle of Archytryst, he was wounded and nearly dead. Ismay led his horse down into a little dell, and there rolled aside a great stone to reveal a spring, from which she gave him a drink and bathed his wounds. He recovered, and since then the well has been a source of help and blessing. It's not too clear from the song, but that is the real story."

"But if he recovered, why is the song called 'Ismay's Sorrow'?"

"Because although she loved him dearly, Polyno became her life's bane. Out of jealousy, he slew her lover Arnat and flung his body into the sea. That is why, if there is sorrow or danger in the land, Ismay's well often becomes salty."

As Ariel spoke, the road descended into a hollow filled with graceful trees. At the bottom, beside the road, they found a well surrounded by a low stone wall. By it, under an arbour, stood a bench. The place was very quiet, still and old.

They had just stopped at the well when there was a stirring in the shadows at one end of the bench, and an incredibly old man hobbled out to meet them. He was wrinkled and brown and bent, but from deep in the folds of his face his two eyes shone out like stars. He smiled warmly in greeting.

"Welcome, travellers," he said. "Have you come to taste the waters of Ismay?"

"I have tasted, Father," replied Ariel, "many years ago. But my companion would like to taste."

"Bless you, my dear, that's right," he said smiling at Elena. "It used to be that every young girl would come and taste the water before her twelfth birthday and have her fortune told. There's blessings in it, you know. But they don't do so much anymore," he said sadly. " 'Tis most often salt now, and so they would prefer to think it lies."

"But I have heard there *is* some danger in the land," said Ariel.

"Ay, that's it, there is," said the old man. "There is. But here, my dear," he went on, "you must try the water for yourself. Come."

But Elena hung back. "I don't know how old I am," she said. "I might be more than twelve."

The old man stopped and studied her for a moment, and then said, "You haven't caught a lover yet, have you?"

Elena flushed hotly and muttered, "No."

"Then it's soon enough," said the old man. "Come."

He led her away from the well to a small shelter nearby among the trees. Within the shelter stood a brazier on a tripod.

"Stand here by the fire," said the old man. "Before the tasting, you must be fumed." So saying, he drew out a handful of herbs and cast them onto the glowing coals. Instantly, Elena was enveloped in a cloud of pungent smoke that went up her nose and made her eyes water. When the smoke cleared and she was able to see again, the old man produced a heavy pendant and said, "Now put this on, and we'll go taste the water."

"What is it?" asked Elena, gazing at the disc. It was made of bone, carved and set with mother-of-pearl.

"Ismay's charm," replied the old man. "She made it herself, hundreds and hundreds of years ago. It draws the truth to those who wear it." As they walked back to the well, Elena felt very solemn and self-conscious with the weight of the charm upon her chest.

At the well's edge, the old man handed her a cup on a slender cord, and said, "Draw a draught, daughter, and see what your life will be."

Obediently, Elena let the cup down into the well. It took a long time to reach the water. When at last she drew it up again, full, she glanced questioningly at the old man.

"Taste, taste," he urged her. "It is your future."

Boldly then, Elena raised the cup and tasted. The water was clear and silvery and icy cold.

"Salt or sweet?" asked the old man eagerly.

"Sweet," said Elena. "Sweet. It tastes of apples."

"Sweet, is it?" said the old man delightedly. "Then a sweet life you'll have for sure, my dear, and a rare one too, these days. Now cast out the draught on this stone here, and I'll riddle some more for you."

With a toss of her hand, Elena sent the rest of the cupful splashing at the old man's feet, where it made a dark pattern on the stone. The man bent to study it, and after a long moment straightened with a look of joy in his eyes.

"Maid," he said, "this be a fair day for you and me, and a fair day too for Estria. You are a Daughter of Ismay."

"A Daughter of Ismay?" said Elena in confusion. "What do you mean?"

"They are a special few, the Daughters," said the old man simply. "You are one. Some are healers, some read dreams, some do nothing but tend the fire and children. But all the Daughters have the power of an open heart to open hearts around them. That is how they help."

Elena stared at the old man in bewilderment, and then looked about for Ariel. He had disappeared.

"Ay," said the old man, "now, I have three Words for you, Daughter. The first one is this: There is wisdom for you in the moon." He fixed Elena with a piercing look. "Mind, I don't say worship or slavery, but wisdom."

Elena nodded.

"Next," he went on, "remember that the sweetest rose in the garden has the sharpest thorns. And the third Word is: Don't speak of this to any but another Daughter."

Elena nodded solemnly again, although she understood little.

"Now, you must learn the knot of Ismay before you go," said the old man. "Watch closely." He pulled a length of cord from his pocket and carefully folded the ends together in a complex knot. "This knot binds all the Daughters and Ismay in one, see?" he said. "Now, you show me."

When at last she had successfully tied the knot, he placed the cord around her neck and said, "Bless you, Daughter. May your work go well. Now go down the road a step. Your companion is waiting for you there."

Light-headed, Elena walked down the road, the light of the setting sun in her eyes. When she came upon Ariel sitting by the side of the road, he studied her carefully for a moment.

At last he said, simply, "Sweet?"

Elena nodded. "Sweet."

9

Singing for Supper

They camped that night on a hill within sight of Rakhbad. Elena's sleep was filled with vivid dreams. She rode endlessly through a desert night on the back of a black-maned lion, coming at dawn to an oasis where she was met by an immensely tall woman robed in white. In the dream, Elena wanted to speak to the woman, but her tongue would not obey her. Instead, they gazed wordlessly at each other, and the silence seemed full of meaning.

When she awoke the dream was still very strong in her, and she was certain it was bound up with the Well of Ismay and the Daughters. She wanted to talk to Ariel about it but she remembered the old man's words: Don't speak of this to any but another Daughter.

It made her feel strange to have such a secret from Ariel. Perhaps from everyone. The old man had said that Daughters were rare. She might never meet one. Then she thought of Ariel and his secret: she had lived with him and travelled with him for years, and never in that time had he breathed a hint about the Brotherhood. The Brotherhood of the Silent Heart. Nor had he mentioned it since they had left the mill at Ballafan. But apparently she was now a part of the Brotherhood, just as she was suddenly a Daughter of Ismay.

But she didn't feel any different. She felt just like herself. Except that the tension of a secret inside made her feel light-footed and careful, like a tight-rope dancer.

As she was thinking this and folding her blanket, Ariel suddenly stooped over and muttered in her ear, "There's riders coming. Tuck your cord away."

There was only time for her to obey before three mounted soldiers came whirling up the road. With a glittering flash and a thunder of hooves, they passed by and Elena was left staring foolishly at Ariel.

Without looking at her, he said quietly, "It's best not to show the knot unless you think there's another Daughter present. Come now, let's be off."

When they stood at last in the crowded square by the Great East Gate, Elena felt a kind of excitement take hold of her. She had been in great cities before—perhaps in Rakhbad as well, although she could not remember it, and she loved the push and noise of them, the strange mixture of exotic and repulsive smells, the amazing assortment of people who always collected in them. She knew too that every city has its own flavour, and she had begun to feel the character of Rakhbad before they had even entered the gate. It had a kind of tension she had never felt before.

"Well," said Ariel as they gazed about them, "we need a place to stay. We'll see if Netta still has her inn by Potter's Well."

Netta's inn, the Silver Dolphin, was a low, rambling building not far from the East Gate. Netta herself was just passing inside the entranceway, carrying two buckets of soapy water towards the stairs, when Ariel caught sight of her.

"Hello, mistress!" he called.

"Just be a minute, master," she replied without looking around. "Gentlemen waiting for their baths." And she disappeared up the stairs.

While she was gone, Elena gazed about her with great curiosity. The Silver Dolphin Inn was very busy. To the right of the entrance way was a common room full of people seated at trestle tables, eating. Two serving lads kept running back and forth to the kitchen and the tap-room as the guests called for more to eat and drink; from the kitchen itself there came a continual bustle and clatter, as well as a rich blend of cooking smells.

Elena had just begun to take these sights in when Netta returned, her buckets empty. "Now then, master—and mistress," she added, glancing at Elena, "what would it be?"

"A room, mistress," replied Ariel. "If you have one. And food."

Netta squinted at Ariel. She was a short, red-headed woman with a shrewd face. "Ay," she said, "you can have both, so long as you are honest. Do I know you?"

"I don't know if you do, ma'am," replied Ariel humbly. "I've stayed here before, though."

The landlady studied him closely for a minute. "Yes, you have," she agreed. "By the day or by the week, then?"

"By the week," said Ariel.

"Three silvers the pair of you, two meals a day and a bath a week thrown in."

"Three silvers!" said Ariel. "It's very dear."

"Too dear," agreed Netta. "But so are bread and soap and firewood."

"Could we work for it?" asked Ariel. "We can sing and play."

"Minstrels, are you?" She glanced at their packs. "All right, you can try your stuff with them," she said, nodding her head towards the common room. "If they like you, you can stay. You can stow your traps in there." She pointed to a small storage room. "And after you sing, you'll get your supper."

Ariel and Elena slung their packs into the little room and prepared to entertain the inn's guests. "There's no room to move," said Ariel, as he took out his flute, "so we'll do songs, and tales if they'll listen. But we'll start with songs." And they went quietly into the common room.

The guests had mostly finished eating by now, and were leaning back and lighting pipes and calling for more drink. Ariel threaded his way through to the far end, and sat on the vacant corner of a table. He made room for Elena, and put his flute to his lips.

The first few notes came almost at random, but as the hubbub around them subsided and people turned to watch, Ariel's fingers settled upon a tune and began to play in earnest. It was a hard, bright song about the sea, one that Elena did not know all the words to, and so instead of singing, she clapped and whistled where she could.

When the sea shanty was over there was polite applause, but the guests were still more curious than enthusiastic. Ariel nodded to Elena. " 'Two Red Shoes,' " he said, and began to play the ballad. This was a song Elena knew well, but she was still surprised when the guests lustily joined in at the first chorus. Ariel had chosen well.

After that it was easy. Their audience settled in for an evening of music, and Ariel and Elena enjoyed themselves singing and playing. The only unsteady point for Elena was when Ariel called for "Ismay's Sorrow." For no reason that she could understand, she felt suddenly weak and hollow, and the strange old, almost meaningless words of the song nearly moved her to tears.

When they at last took their leave of the company and made their way from the room, to many a rough and friendly pat on the back, Netta met them at the door and said simply, "Your dinner is in the kitchen. Pym will show you your room when you've eaten." Elena was not too tired to feel a triumphant glow at the words.

10

Reports and Surmises

Elena awoke alone in their little room beside the stable. She stretched comfortably and, noticing the angle of the sun, realized it was near midday. Ariel was sitting on a bench outside the kitchen door. "Did you eat?" he asked, squinting up at her.

"I slept through breakfast," she said.

"Then let's have lunch," he replied. "While we are in the City of the King, we must try to live like kings and eat three meals a day. Come."

Leading her from the innyard, he set off at a rapid pace through the maze of the city. At last they came to the foot of a high tower which appeared to be part of an ancient wall or battlement, though it was now surrounded by common houses. There, in a deep archway, a wooden door led them to the tower stairs, which coiled upward, it seemed, forever. They climbed in puffing silence until at last they emerged in the bare, sun-washed chamber at the top. Chamber was perhaps not the right word, for although it was roofed, the walls were only waist-high, giving a splendid view in all directions.

"There," said Ariel, "a fine place for lunch—and a council." Sitting with his back against the parapet, he drew forth the lunch he had brought, and said grimly: "I heard terrible news this morning."

The gravity of Ariel's tone sent a chill running down Elena's back. "What is it?" she asked.

"The Black Priests control the Palace," said Ariel. "The King has not been seen for a month."

"But—"

"I have this from my friend Liander, who works in the stables of the King. Akheem has gone into the Red Chamber, and none may see him there but the Priests. Messages from his ministers are ignored. The Priests have gathered more and more of the Palace under their dominion. They issue orders in the King's name. They divide the nobles with gossip and dispute. They rule the servants with fear and greed."

Elena said, "What can we do?"

"There are still some who are loyal to the King, who see the Black Priests for what they are and resist them as they can," replied Ariel. "Most of the Palace Guard, I think. Good soldiers wouldn't trust a priest, not these priests, at any rate. Some of the nobles, too. A few of the ministers are faithful yet, but their scribes and functionaries are cowed, and so they have no power. The Priests, you see, have had a fine time unravelling the court. The best we can do now is knit together what is left, and hope the King will reappear."

"And if he doesn't?" asked Elena.

"Our other task," said Ariel, "is to watch the life of Prince Yadral. He is the only heir to the throne, and his life these days is probably not worth a pile of straw. Fortunately," Ariel went on, "he is not at court just now. Liander says he is paying a lengthy visit to his aunt, the Duchess of Moulton, on the far side of the Western Mountains. That is good, but all the same, I will send a message to a Brother there to watch him."

"And . . . Barkat?" said Elena at length.

"Liander knew nothing of Barkat. I fear he is dead."

They finished their small lunch and gazed over the parapet at the city below. Somewhere amid the jumble of houses a peddler called, his voice small and distant.

"There," said Ariel, pointing. "That is the Palace. The

large gate in front is Minifer's Gate. Behind is the Park Royal. The low building on this side is the barracks of the Palace Guard. The other side is the stables, where Liander lives. Beyond the palace grounds, on the far side of the bay, are the High Hills.''

"But they are low," said Elena with a laugh. "Barely hills at all.''

"So it seems," said Ariel wryly, "but great lords and ladies live there in fine stone houses, and that makes them high.''

"Oh.'' After a pause Elena said, "Ariel? How will we do this knitting?''

"I don't know," said Ariel. "By listening and waiting and talking. By being good servants of the King. I have other friends to see who will tell me more.''

"Brothers?''

"Some of them.''

"Is Liander in the Brotherhood?''

"It's better that you not know," said Ariel. "The Priests are looking for the Brotherhood. They have heard of it, and no doubt they feel it, too. Their own fear blinds them, of course. Probably what they are looking for is more like themselves than the Brotherhood, but they are dangerous and not unperceptive. If you ever meet one, it would be best if you had nothing to conceal.''

"But I know about you. Isn't that dangerous?''

"Ay," said Ariel with a laugh. "Very.''

11

The Threat of the Twisted Hand

That evening at dinner-time, while the other guests ate, Ariel and Elena sat in a quiet corner near the common room, working out their turn for the night.

"We did well with songs yesterday," said Ariel, "but we'll try some variety tonight. Do you remember the 'Lay of Edward Bold'?"

"I remember the first song," said Elena doubtfully. " 'Edward Bold A'Down the Lea,' isn't it?"

"Right," said Ariel. "Then I tell the part, you know, about him riding to see the Maid Lucinda—'The flash of steel, the thunder of hooves, His horse did gleam like copper fine'—and when he splashes across the ford· at Waterlost, you sing 'A Maiden Like an Elm Tree Fair.' It goes like this—" and he hummed the tune.

"Oh, yes," said Elena. "I remember."

"Then comes a long part where you don't do anything. I say some poetry, then—" Ariel stopped suddenly and Elena became aware of a stranger a few paces off. He was a thin yellowish man in a tattered sea cloak, his head bent to catch their words. Now he looked up, smiled ingratiatingly, and said, "Good evening, sir! I have just come from across the sea. Is the—is the landlord about?"

Ariel nodded. "It would be the landlady, Mistress Netta, you require."

"Of course, of course, the land*lady*," said the stranger. "In the kitchen, would she be?"

"I couldn't say," said Ariel. "But you have only to call."

"Oh, no need for that," said the stranger, coming a step closer and lowering his voice. "No need for that. I like to *travel* quietly." A prickle of suspicion ran up Elena's neck. "Yes," he said, "I *travel* very quietly indeed." And he nodded significantly.

"Ah," said Ariel gravely, "some men do." There was a brief pause. Elena could feel the two men studying each other, weighing the possibilities. "Well," said Ariel at last, leaning forward and dropping his voice, "since you travel, as you say, quietly," and he looked about to be sure they were unobserved, then leaned even nearer. The stranger edged closer too, an eager light in his eyes. "Since you wish to *travel* quietly," said Ariel, "beware of the cabbage pickles here, sir. They're terrible for gas."

The stranger started back, mingled rage and consternation on his face, but Ariel merely gave him a solemn nod, and turning to Elena, said, "It's time for us to sing."

Applause greeted them in the common room. Bowing graciously, they seated themselves, and straightaway began the "Lay of Edward Bold." Elena had finished the first song and was listening to Ariel recite the next verses, when she suddenly felt a queer uneasiness steal over her. Glancing up, she saw the stranger, his eyes narrowed to bitter slits, standing at the far end of the room. Thrust forth from his cloak, his right hand was twisted in a peculiar gesture of hatred.

Elena felt the anxiety surge upwards in her until she knew she must run away or be sick on the spot. But there was no escape. Even as she watched those glittering, malevolent eyes, she heard Ariel giving her the cue for "A Maiden Like An Elm Tree Fair."

Not knowing whether her voice would come or not, Elena

opened her mouth to sing, but at that moment several things happened. Ariel stamped. It appeared to be a brisk introduction to the song, but Elena had never heard him use it before. At the same instant, Pym, hurrying into the hall, tripped and fell headlong, sending a great pitcher of beer full in the face of the stranger.

The uproar was tremendous. The stranger, when he had caught his breath and spat the beer out of his mouth, screeched incoherently, while Pym shouted almost as loudly that he had been tripped. Those close by denied this hotly, but those farther away, who had seen nothing, shouted that it was a shame to play such tricks on a boy, and a waste of good beer at that.

It might have all come to blows if Netta had not appeared on the scene and quickly tugged and pushed the room back into order. Only the stranger would not be mollified. Refusing all offers of towels, fresh clothes and a bath, he stormed away into the evening, leaving behind him a trail of oaths and beer.

Late that night, Elena and Ariel lay in their room by the stable. Through the window poured the light of a waxing moon. When he had blown out the candle, Ariel had shown by a sign that they were not to talk, and so Elena had lain in silence, looking at the silver moon sail across the sky.

Now, at the sound of Ariel stirring, she looked over and saw him sitting up, looking back at her. With a smile he beckoned her to sit close to him by the window.

"Do you understand?" he asked in a whisper. "That was a spy."

Elena nodded.

"This one was clumsy and ill-prepared, but others may come who are more subtle. *Will* come, certainly. We must be very careful."

"How did you know he was a spy?"

Ariel paused. Around them, all was silent. Then, some

streets away, a donkey brayed. "Mind and heart," said Ariel. "He tried to tell my mind one thing while my heart heard another."

"What did he try to tell you?"

"He tried to say he was from the Brotherhood. 'I've come from across the sea,' he said, which is one way of saying 'I have gone beyond my self, I am landlocked no longer.' But my heart heard a bitter selfish man, who has not even begun *that* voyage. And besides, this inn is far from the harbour, and so his sea cloak and his double meaning were out of place. A true Brother would have noticed that."

"But they must know about us if—"

"They suspect, perhaps," said Ariel. "I think he came here and simply tried his trick on the first stranger he met. They have no reason to suppose us other than we seem."

"But you broke his spell," protested Elena.

"Did I?"

"Well, you stamped."

"And Pym tripped, and Netta filled a pitcher with good rich Northland beer. If the stranger got wet, it was the consequence of his own ill will. Don't you know," he said, "whatever you give comes back to you? Ill will, good will, rough words or gentle, we are always paid back in our own coin."

Elena pondered this for a moment. "What was he trying to give *us*?" she asked.

Ariel chuckled. "Perhaps he was trying to give us indigestion. It was silly of me to play that cabbage pickle trick on him. But remember, Elena, these men have no power without your fear. That is where their strength begins. And if the pure flame burning *here*," he said, touching her over the heart, "remains unshaken, their 'magic' as they think it has no power. Remember that."

Long after, when Ariel had gone to sleep, Elena lay in the

darkness, eyes wide. The night was growing old, and the moon had sunk to one corner of the window, but she could not sleep. In her breast where Ariel had touched her so lightly, there now burned a steady fire.

12

Knots and Nobility

When Elena woke the next morning, Ariel was sitting on his bed mending a pair of tights. "We must put our gear in order," he said as she sat up. "We have an important performance tonight."

"Here?" she asked, rolling out of bed.

"No, not at the inn. Tonight we play for lords and ladies, at the home of Count Fabiad in the High Hills."

Elena's eyes widened. "What will we be doing?"

"A little of everything, I should think. The Count and Countess are having a dinner party in their garden, a very beautiful setting if it has not changed. We must be prepared with stories, songs, juggling, tumbling, anything that may be called for."

Elena had by this time begun to lay out her performing clothes: her tights, her soft snug tumbler's shirt, short skirt and slippers. The tights and shirt were midnight blue, and the ribbons for her hair and slippers were red. The colours were understated, but Ariel had taught her long ago that bright colours both attract and distract. If the audience was already gathered, a performer could keep his costume simple.

"You have worked there before, then," she said.

Ariel nodded, biting off a thread. "When the old Count was alive," he said. "Often."

"Are they—" Elena was going to ask: are they friends, enemies of the Black Priests, have they seen the King, but

Ariel held up his hand at the sound of approaching footsteps. There was a shadow outside the door as Netta strode by, apparently towards the stables.

When she had passed, Ariel laid his finger beside his nose and said in a droll manner, "Have you seen the harbour yet, my dear?"

"No," said Elena with a grin.

"Splendid. When you have finished with your traps, we shall stroll down and take it in." And he honoured her with a comic bow.

Of all the cities, towns and villages she had visited, Elena loved those beside the sea the best. Boats of any kind could make her blood sing. The salt smell of the air and the lazy swell of the harbour always made her feel light and restless, as though she could fly for a thousand leagues across the water, skimming and dipping over the wavetops like a gull.

The harbour at Rakhbad was no exception. The land side was jammed with warehouses, fishmongers, shipwrights, chandlers, sail makers, coopers, carters, inns for sailors. And the sea side was jammed with ships. The sight of it filled her with a restless longing for something that she could not put a name to.

She and Ariel strolled along the docks watching the bustle and activity of the port. Now and then the way would be blocked and they would have to stand aside for a cart laden with bales and boxes, or step around a barrel of salt fish, or over great coils and skeins of sea cable. And always, there was the smell of the sea and the call of seabirds around them.

At last they came to the end of the docks, where there were only one or two small fishing boats tied up, and all was quiet. Sitting on an old timber, they had a fine view of the bay before them. To their right lay the port and the city; to their left, the mouth of the bay and the open sea. Directly before them, across the bay, they could see the mansions and fine gardens of the nobility spread along the High Hills.

"Count Fabiad's house is there, by the water," said Ariel, pointing. "You can see grey columns."

"Yes," replied Elena. "I see it."

"The dinner will likely be below the house. There is a broad open place in the garden there. And," he added with a smile, "we shall be working on the softest turf in Estria."

"Are they—" Elena again tried to frame the question she had begun in their room by the stable. "Are they loyal to the King?"

Ariel bent and picked up a piece of broken cord that lay beside his foot. "I believe so," he said. "But it is difficult to tell. About anyone. Almost everyone will swear their allegiance to the King, but in the end it is only their actions which tell you where their hearts lie. I knew Count Fabiad's father, the old Count, very well." He idly knotted the cord as he spoke. "There was a bond between us of trust and friendship. But I scarcely know his son. I think he is good. But by all reports, he takes little part in the court. He seems content to leave the Palace to itself."

Elena pondered this. "Why are we bothering to play there, then?"

Ariel tugged a knot into shape. "Because we will be handsomely paid, and because whatever may be, we will undoubtedly learn more than at Mistress Netta's inn. Now, what's this knot?" he asked, showing her the cord.

Elena looked. "Swindler's knot."

"Swindler's knot," repeated Ariel with some satisfaction. "It looks good, but it doesn't hold. In the Parsat Islands, they use knots to write letters, did you know? What's this one?"

"Hunter's knot."

"Yes, because the knot slides up to catch whatever is in the loop. And this?"

"That's a true knot."

"Because it holds and never changes," agreed Ariel. "This?"

"Fisherman's twist," said Elena.

"Yes," said Ariel. "Also called a quick knot, because it can be undone very easily, even in the freezing sea. Do you know this one?"

Elena studied the knot. "I've never seen that one before."

"In Parsat they call this the door knot, also the knot of freedom. I don't know why. It's made like this."

For a long time they sat on the old timber by the edge of the sea, their low voices murmuring over the knots while the water swelled and sucked beneath them. When a knot was new to Elena, Ariel patiently showed her how it was tied.

"You never know," he said with a smile. "You might wish to send me a letter from Parsat one day."

"How would you sign your name?"

"Well," said Ariel, "that would depend. You could use this one," and his fingers lightly brushed her shirt, under which dangled the hidden knot of Ismay. "I would use . . ." He thought for a moment. "Probably the fisherman's twist."

"Why?" demanded Elena.

Ariel laughed. "Because it is so easily undone."

At last the sun began to dip towards the High Hills, and it was time for them to go. As they stood up Ariel suddenly said, "It could be anything we are looking for, you know. Anything. We must keep our eyes and ears wide open."

13

The Face at the Window

Hastening through the late afternoon streets towards the High Hills, Elena felt the magic of what she called a "high performance" settling over her. It was a peculiar mixture of tension, excitement, stillness, awareness and elation that always filled her when she worked a special occasion. Not that she had a reverence for nobility, but she knew that the richness and fineness of court life made her perform as she never could at the Silver Dolphin.

As they walked, the streets gradually transformed. Narrow, crowded lanes gave way to broad avenues, almost deserted. Shops disappeared, to be replaced by high walls overhung by flowering trees. From time to time a carriage rumbled by, drawn by the most elegant horses in coloured harness.

"This is Count Fabiad's," said Ariel when they came to a particularly ornate gateway. It was a deep vaulted passage, barred at the inner end by great iron gates, and carved all about in the shapes of trees, flowers and strange creatures. At the very top of the arch hung a stone relief of a leaping fish, which Ariel said was the Fabiad sign.

They did not enter by the large gate at the end of the passage, but went instead to a small barred doorway at the side and called through it for the gatekeeper. After a long wait, a small white-haired old man appeared at the grating and asked in a hoarse voice what they wanted.

"His lordship bids us come to entertain his guests," Ariel told him.

"What's your names?" asked the old man.

"Ariel and Elena."

"All right. Just a minute." And he vanished into the darkness, reappearing in a moment with a ring of keys, and unlocked the gate. "This way, please," he said, and led them, with a curious shuffling step, down a narrow passage and out into the sunshine on the other side.

"Now don't take the road," said the old man. "It's too long. Just follow this stone path here, it'll take you directly to the main house, and then you go around the *left* side. Left, that's this one," he said, tugging forcefully at Ariel's left sleeve, "and ask anyone you see for Riddle. Riddle, d'you understand? He'll show you what to do."

"Yes," said Ariel. "Thank you."

"This path. Left side. Riddle. Remember now."

And when they set off down the path, the old man watched them until they were out of sight, to be sure they didn't get lost.

The stone pathway curved through a quiet, open forest. The trunks of the trees reached high and dark into the canopy above, and delicate, star-shaped flowers nestled about their roots. In the distance, a cuckoo called. "It's beautiful," said Elena, gazing about as they went.

"Yes," said Ariel, "beautiful and very old. And once," he said, glancing around, "very large indeed."

"It seems very large now," said Elena. They had been walking for some minutes, and still there was no sign of the house.

"Well, it *is* large," conceded Ariel, "but once it was even larger. In the old days, when there were just the twelve noble families, they each had estates here in the High Hills that had fields and parks and woods stretching on for miles. Now it's different, of course. Smaller and more crowded.''

As Ariel spoke, the house of the Fabiads appeared through the trees ahead. It was a rambling old house, built of rough grey stone and mostly covered with ivy. They emerged from the trees quite near to it. Turning left as they had been directed, they made their way towards the back.

As they walked between flower beds and the vine-covered walls, Elena glanced at a window above her, and was startled by the sight of a pale face peering intently down at them. The instant she looked up, the face disappeared as though it did not want to be observed, but it left a vivid impression in her mind: a thin face with two vertical lines between the eyebrows—lines of worry. She was on the point of mentioning it to Ariel when they turned a corner and barely avoided a young girl staggering under the weight of two huge baskets.

"I beg your pardon," said Ariel courteously. "Could you direct us to Master Riddle?"

"I can do better than that," the girl replied. "If you walk along with me, I'll take you to him."

"Then let us help you with the baskets," said Ariel.

"I won't say no. They are a little heavy and that's the truth. There's always so much to do the day of a dinner party. Is that what brought you here?"

"Yes, it is," Ariel said. He and Elena had fallen in on either side of the girl, each lending a hand with the baskets, filled, Elena saw, with china plates. "We've come to entertain. This is Elena and I am Ariel."

"And I am Lou," the girl answered. "Riddle will be pleased to see you. He was saying this morning what a stroke of luck it was you had turned up. Have you been away, then?"

She spoke with an engaging directness that made Elena smile. "We've been travelling for years," she said.

"Imagine! For years? You must have stories!"

They walked across a broad, green lawn behind the house, and under a huge oak tree found Master Riddle supervising the laying of the table.

He was a short, broad man, and bald as an egg. He stood by the table and gave orders to a flurry of servants in a high, wheezing voice.

"Master Riddle?" said Ariel with a bow. "Ariel."

"Ariel!" said Riddle, turning with a sudden smile. "Master Ariel! How are you?" And he shook him warmly by the hand. Then, before Ariel could reply, he said to Lou, "All right, now lay out those plates, and make sure they are dusted as you go. When that is done, go and help Osim with the chairs. Thank you. Now, Ariel?"

"Never better," replied Ariel, smiling as well, "Riddle, this is Elena. We work together."

"A pleasure, mistress," said Riddle, bending over her hand. "A pleasure. Ariel, when I heard you would be here tonight, I thought it must be someone else, some other Ariel. We must find time for a talk."

"Gladly," said Ariel. "How will the evening run?"

Riddle mopped his brow. "The guests arrive within the hour, a small gathering, as you can see," he said, indicating the table which was set with perhaps three dozen places. "They will assemble on the South Terrace and after some light refreshment there, Lady Fabiad will lead them here at dusk." Glancing casually about, Riddle added confidentially, "I must tell you, one of His Grace's guests has a particular desire not to be recognized, Ariel. I know we can trust your discretion." Wordlessly, Ariel inclined his head in reply.

"The dinner runs the normal courses," Riddle went on. "You will, of course, be at liberty throughout the evening. Whatever suits the mood. When the meal is finished, seek out me or Basset in the Servants' Hall."

"I understand," replied Ariel.

"Now, you must excuse me, Ariel, Elena. I hope we'll have some time when this is done. In the meantime, the gardener's cottage is at your disposal." And with a bow, he turned and hurried away, calling out as he did so, "Thabo, where are the candles? Hurry!"

As they slowly walked away from the table and the last minute bustle of servants, Elena noticed a small and secret smile on Ariel's lips. "An unknown guest!" he said quietly. "This might prove more valuable than we thought."

14

The Stranger Wrapped in Grey

The gardener's cottage was set in a nearby hollow, screened from the main house by trees and a thick flowering hedge. It was a stout stone house with a thatched roof, so crowded about with arbours and planters and cold frames that it was difficult to tell where the garden left off and the house began. Elena liked it instantly.

"Hullo," said Ariel, as they came to the door of the cottage. "Someone's put a rose bush here. Elmet would have liked that. He was the gardener here for many years, until he died. He was a Brother, too."

There was no answer to their knock, and so they entered, but found no sign of the present gardener. "Likely sent away," said Ariel. "The fewer prying eyes the better, if there's really something up."

Elena shrugged her pack off onto a bunk by the window and said, "But if they don't want prying eyes, why are *we* here?"

"There are several possibilities," Ariel said, undoing his own pack, "and they may all be right. First, it may be that Lord and Lady Fabiad simply cannot face the thought of a dinner party without some diversion, no matter what clandestine scheme is afoot. Newly arrived in the city and untouched as yet by the intrigues which rise and fall here daily, we are chosen as 'safe.' Or, it may be—in fact, it is quite likely—

that not everyone invited tonight is in on the secret, whatever it is. In that case, we may be a sort of camouflage, to help make everything seem normal. Or, and this is a possibility which I think has not even occurred to our worthy Riddle, it may be that *we* are part of the secret."

Elena pulled on her tumbling shirt. "What do you mean?"

"Well," said Ariel, getting out his own tumbling clothes, "if Lord Fabiad's guest *really* doesn't want to be recognized, not by anybody, he's only got to stay out of the way, doesn't he? Going to dinner parties, however select, is a funny way of hiding. So, if he's here, he wants to see and be seen by somebody else here. And we're here. So it might be us."

Elena considered this gravely, and then said, "But this guest might not have anything to do with . . . with our . . . "

"With our task?" said Ariel. "Quite right. The chances are ten to one this is some petty family matter of no consequence at all to any but those involved. But remember that in court life, everything revolves around the King, no matter how remote or trivial. And since we have nothing to go on now, anything we learn will be an improvement."

By this time they had both changed into their performing clothes. Ariel took his southern double pipe from his pack, and Elena picked up finger cymbals and a small drum, then followed him from the cottage.

As they emerged from the trees and made their way up the lawn towards the South Terrace, they saw Riddle, silhouetted by the evening sun, casting an enormous shadow towards them. He stood alone, surveying his work, allowing himself a moment of stillness before the guests arrived. When he saw them coming, he nodded, turned and went inside.

The terrace was long and broad, covered with potted plants and flowers. It offered a magnificent view of the grounds and the quiet greeny-blue waters of the bay. Along one edge a tall hedge had been clipped to form a number of alcoves, where groups of two or three people might sit quietly and talk.

"Here," said Ariel, indicating one. "We shall play from here, until they all arrive. Then we can move about."

They did not wait long. With a gust of laughter, four people swept through the double doors and onto the terrace. Instantly Ariel struck up a lively air on his pipes, and Elena followed him, tapping her drum and touching her cymbals.

It was obvious that two of the people were the Lord and Lady Fabiad. The Count, smiling and assured, stood a head taller than the lady he escorted, who was a brown-skinned Altan, dressed in a gold and silver version of her native dress. The Countess, tall and blonde, dressed all in blue with a gleaming silver moon at her throat, talked animatedly with an aquiline man who wore the guild robes of a merchant prince of Sumner.

They were soon joined by another couple, ushered out this time by Riddle, and Elena lost count as more guests arrived. When they finished their tune, Ariel nodded and they quietly rose and began to thread their way amongst the people.

Elena always enjoyed this kind of work. The rules were simple: pay attention; don't intrude. Slowly they walked from one group to another, never coming too close, never staying in one place too long, playing softly as though to themselves and for anyone else who cared to listen. The strange thing was that although no word was ever spoken between them, it was at such times as these that Elena and Ariel were closest. Although they had come to play for the people, it was as if the people had disappeared, and they existed in their own private world, a small floating world of music.

Dusk soon began to fall, and Riddle appeared on the terrace to announce that dinner was waiting. Lady Fabiad led the way on the arm of the merchant prince, and the others drifted after, trailing across the broad lawn in their bright and fluttering silks like so many delicate moths.

Ariel and Elena stood at the back of the terrace, watching them. When the last guest had gone, Ariel said, "We have a few minutes. We should go back to the cottage and change our gear."

But as they turned to go, they were startled by a man hurrying from the house across the terrace. He was wearing a long grey cloak and a hood that hid his face entirely. Unaware of their presence, he slipped off the terrace into the gathering shadows below the house.

"Well," said Ariel with a chuckle, "if this is Riddle's secret guest, he needn't fear us recognizing him. A mountaineer's cape like that could cover almost anybody."

Elena agreed; they had seen the secret guest and were certainly no wiser. But she also felt certain that the face concealed by the grey hood was the same as the pale face she had seen earlier at the window.

But who that was, and what his business here was, remained a mystery.

15

Words in Moss Alley

Dinner at Lord Fabiad's was a lengthy affair, made up of many courses, between which the guests would rise from the table and stroll about the gardens in the soft night air, admiring the stars and bobbing lamps of the fishing boats upon the inky waters of the bay. Each new course was signalled by the gentle ringing of silver bells. Ariel and Elena performed while the guests were at table.

Their pace, like that of the meal, was slow and measured. They moved casually from end to end of the long table, singing, playing, slow tumbling, always staying just within the light, working quietly around the tray-laden servers. As they passed, the guests would often turn in their chairs, smiling, to watch them. But there was one who never looked up, though his murmured conversation fell silent at their approach. It was the stranger in the grey cloak.

He sat at one end of the table. His neighbours had been cleverly chosen, for on one side sat an aged and very deaf dowager, and across from him was the Altan lady who, although her smile was very bright, could only speak her own language.

But Elena found the mysterious guest no more compelling than his hostess, Lady Fabiad, who sat at the other end of the table. Each time Elena passed, the Countess made a point of catching her eye and smiling, a quiet smile that bound them together, although they had not yet spoken.

At the end of a particularly long and vigorous tumbling cycle, Elena found herself just beside Lady Fabiad, rising at that moment from the table. Bowing deeply as she had been taught, Elena murmured, "Your servant, my lady."

"And yours, my dear," replied the Countess with a laugh. "What is your name?"

"I am called Elena, my lady."

"And this must be Ariel," she said, turning to him as he came up.

"Your servant, Lady Fabiad," he answered, bowing low.

"I am enjoying your performance very much," she went on. "I hope you will be frequent visitors while you are staying in Rakhbad." Her voice had a peculiar flute-like quality that Elena found appealing; it reminded her of crisp apples savoured in the fall.

"You are most kind, my lady," said Ariel. "The house of Fabiad has ever been gracious and hospitable."

As she turned to go she said: "But do come! I'm sure you have wonderful stories. I should love to hear them." And with a smile, she was gone. Elena was sure, against all reason, that Lady Fabiad's parting smile and last words had been meant for her alone.

Elena and Ariel hurried towards the cottage to exchange their instruments. As they made their way silently down a dark, curving walkway that Ariel called Moss Alley, Elena sensed, rather than saw, Ariel stop short before her.

They stood frozen for a moment, and then Elena heard the murmur of voices. Two men were coming towards them along the alleyway, but just when it seemed they would round the corner and run right into them, they stopped. Then a deep voice said, "My lord, Lord Orrime," and another voice, in muffled tones, said "My lord!" But to Elena's surprise, a third voice spoke, saying "Well met, Orrime, well met." A third person had been waiting just around the corner.

Then the first deep voice spoke again: "My lords, we've not much time. I have disclosed to Orrime your intentions, my lord, and I have told him how he might help you in this plan."

"And your resolve?" said the third voice.

"My lord," said the second, "I am resolved to serve you, but this seems to me a perilous way to go."

"Do you fear for your life?" asked the third voice.

"I fear for yours, my lord, and for your father's."

"Although my father has disowned me for a pack of dogs and cut-throats, I would not willingly imperil his life. What would you counsel?"

"Only caution, my lord."

"That we have taken. When may we have your men?"

"By boat, in three days' time. By land, a week."

"Send for them by boat, then, and bid them land as secretly as may be at Iaspar's Cove. Meet us at Whittuck Crossing, at dawn on the fourth day. Should you be challenged, the password is 'Appin's Will.' Or your sword. Whichever will serve."

"I understand, my lord."

"Now go, and Grace be with you."

Then, after a hasty leavetaking, it seemed that the two had made their way back down the alleyway. For an agonizing moment after that, Elena and Ariel waited to see which way the third would leave, and at last they heard an almost silent tread move slowly away from them.

When they finally dared to stir, Elena discovered she had been clenching her fist tightly about the knot of Ismay, although she could not remember taking it out from its hiding place. Wordlessly, Ariel took her hand and they stole past the meeting place towards the gardener's cottage. There was no need to advise silence.

16

Sudden Favour, Sudden Fall

In the gardener's cottage, Ariel picked up his four-stringed lute, strummed it once, and set it by the door for the next course. Then, he extinguished the small lamp by the window and drew Elena beside him on the bench. He spoke in a voice so low it could not have been understood across the room.

"The password, 'Appin's Will,' " he said. "Appin is an ancient word for fire. But in the high court language it is also part of Prince Yadral's title: Appin bar talib, Protector of the Fire."

"Is it Prince Yadral?" breathed Elena, meaning the grey-cloaked guest.

"I am sure of it," whispered Ariel fiercely. "But he is taking a terrible risk to do this. If the King or the Black Priests knew of it, his life would likely be forfeit."

"What does he plan to do?" asked Elena.

"March on the Palace, it seems. Seize power. But what do *we* plan to do, is the question."

"Shouldn't we help?"

"Maybe," said Ariel. "It's a bold plan, and risks a civil war, though it might work. But a failure would bring catastrophe."

"What should we do, then?"

"I don't know," said Ariel. "I must talk to the Prince, if I can. Or to Lord Fabiad. But it will be difficult to do without alarming them."

"Perhaps you can talk to Riddle," suggested Elena. "He must know something of this."

"You're right," said Ariel. "Yes. I should have thought of that myself."

But though the next course was being brought steaming from the kitchens, and the other servants hovered ready in the edge of the lamplight, Riddle was not to be found.

"That's strange," said Ariel. "He's been practically standing on the table all evening long."

There was no time to worry about Riddle's absence, though, for the course was being served and it was time for them to perform.

Silently, Elena took her place halfway along the table just within the light, and waited. Behind her in the shadows, Ariel strummed his lute and began to play the opening theme of a dance and ballad called "The White Queen in Spring." Elena's cue was fast approaching when she noticed Riddle suddenly appear at one end of the table and urgently whisper in Lord Fabiad's ear. A look of perplexity crossed the Count's face, but he nodded and leaned over to speak to the grey-cloaked figure beside him.

Elena was intensely interested in this, but she could not ignore her cue, and she turned and began to sing. When she turned again, half a minute later, the chair beside Lord Fabiad was empty. The Prince had stolen away.

As the song spiralled to a dramatic climax, Elena was astonished to see the entire company rise to its feet. Suddenly there was silence. All stood, clutching napkins, spoons or glasses, and turned towards Elena.

But it was not Elena at whom they looked. Turning, herself, Elena saw, not two feet away, the King.

He stood leaning on a stick. In his youth, he must have been straight and strong, but now he was bent, caved in upon himself. His broad shoulders and knotted hands only emphasized how thin his long arms were. His hair was lank and grey, and his face haggard, with deep circles under his eyes. But for all that, his glance, as he surveyed the company, was keen and hard as a diamond.

Close behind him, noiseless as shadows, stood three Black Priests, looking distinctly angry.

It was Lord Fabiad who broke the silence. Appearing suddenly beside Elena, he sank to one knee before the King and said, "Your Majesty, an unexpected honour."

Akheem regarded him for a moment, then said in a worn voice, "Rise, Fabiad, rise. And carry on your dinner. Do not stop for me. Only bring me a chair here that I may watch this girl perform."

One of the Priests quickly bent forward to whisper in the King's ear, but at the first hissing sound the King angrily muttered, "Get off!" and thrust him aside with one arm. The Priest staggered back. "Bring me a chair," repeated the King, "and let the feast proceed."

A chair was brought (the same, Elena saw, that had just been vacated by the Prince) and the King sat stiffly. One by one, the guests resumed their seats. As the company came faltering back to life, the King turned to Elena, fixed her with his glance, and nodded, once.

Ariel must have been watching closely from the darkness. At the King's nod he instantly resumed the opening bars of "The White Queen in Spring," and with a deep bow, Elena took up the song. As she did she noticed, almost with surprise, that she felt not the least bit nervous. Instead, she was filled with calm assurance. She could see that the King was ravaged, that he was deeply tired, and that, somehow, he had been cornered by the Priests and held at bay. She knew, or sensed, that he felt bitter and betrayed, and yet she also knew, without knowing how she knew, that the heart of the King was yet true and solid, in spite of all his trials.

As she sang and danced, she felt calmness spreading through and around her, guiding her through "The White Queen." A part of her completely lost itself in the song, so that she performed with a fierce sincerity. But the other part of her watched coolly, it seemed, from a point a little way above her head, and was aware of everything around her—the guests, the comings and goings of the servants, Ariel, the King, and the Priests.

She was particularly aware of the Priests. Cloaked in black with pale reptilian faces, they remained behind the King, freezing with their glances any servant bold enough to offer them chairs, food or drink. Once, at the beginning of a dance passage, she saw them draw together, though she could not tell which one was speaking. When she could look again, one Priest had slipped away into the darkness, leaving only two to hover at the shoulders of the King like ominous clouds.

This worried Elena. She had no way of knowing where the Priest had gone, but somewhere in the darkness around them the Prince might be hiding, and it would not do for the two to meet. But there was nothing she could do, and so she merely sang and danced, putting all her power into the performance. She did not know it herself then, but that night she sang more wildly and sweetly, and danced more strongly and gracefully, than she had ever done before.

When at last she sank to the grass and the last notes of the lute died away, there was a moment of silence. Then a single person began clapping. Looking up, Elena found the King leaning forward in his chair, applauding her, while the guests looked on, transfixed.

"What is your name, girl?" asked the King.

"Elena, your Majesty."

"Elena, I give you leave of the Palace. Come tomorrow at the seventh hour." With that, the King rose and walked down towards the beach. Without looking back he called out, "Fabiad! You are a loyal subject and a good host. Thank you for indulging one more old guest.'' And he vanished into the darkness, trailing the shadowy Priests behind him.

The thought that there should have been three Priests, and that one was still missing, flickered briefly through Elena's mind, but a tremendous surge of elation swept it from her, and she turned towards the gardener's cottage. Leave of the Palace! And she was to see the King tomorrow evening! She must find Ariel at once.

Her way was barred by a flock of guests, full of praise for her talents. It was some time before she could politely edge away from the circle and sprint to the cottage.

She was halfway down inky-dark Moss Alley, her mind full of her good fortune, when she noticed a movement on the path. It was too late. There was a sudden flurry before her, a brutal blow to her forehead, and Elena, with a groan, tumbled into darkness.

17

Alone and Friendless

When Elena opened her eyes it was morning. She guessed from the light that it was about five o'clock. She lay crumpled under a hedge with leaves in her hair, a lump like an egg on her forehead and a terrible headache.

At first she lay still, with her cheek pressed against a root, and stared blankly at the ground. Everything was intensely quiet. After a moment she rolled over and thought: *Where's Ariel?*

Elena struggled to her feet and staggered back down the moss walkway to the lawn. The glittering dinnerware and festive lamplight were gone now, along with the people. Long rays of morning sun revealed only a row of wooden tables, rather plain and homely without their fine linen covers.

She turned towards the gardener's cottage. *Perhaps he's waiting for me there*, she thought. And then: *I'm thirsty.* As she passed the spot where she had lain all night, she saw deep gouges in the moss, as if a struggle had taken place there, but her aching mind was unable to make any sense of what she saw.

At the cottage was a scene Elena could not at first understand. Trailed across the doorstep like a bright silk banner was one of her own hairbands. But as she stared dully at it, she saw that it was torn and stained, and that the step also bore a broad dark stain. She bent to peer more closely and realized that it was blood.

She pushed through the half-open door into the cottage. A scene of terrible disorder met her. Her pack—and Ariel's too— had been torn open and scattered, tables overturned, shelves swept clear. And across it all lay a trail of blood.

After a moment she went out again, and stood helplessly in the sunlight. *What should I do?* she thought, but no answer came. She had hoped to find Ariel, but Ariel was not there. Something had happened. He was gone. Hurt somewhere. *Or dead.*

She saw that the rosebush by the door was smashed, and bent to straighten it. Her fingers were clumsy though, and she slipped and pricked herself deeply on the thorns. She watched numbly as bright beads of blood formed on her fingers. Then she brushed them off and stood up.

Lady Fabiad, she thought. *I should look for Lady Fabiad.*

As she turned in the direction of the big house, she saw a rain barrel half-hidden in the bushes.

She went to it, and finding it brim-full, gratefully scooped up handfuls of cool water. She drank deeply, and then gingerly bathed her face, so that some of the morning light and air came in to her. Refreshed a little, with face and hands dripping, she leaned against the cottage and tried to think.

She could not believe anything had happened to Ariel. Or she would not. But the torn apart packs, the stillness and the blood allowed her no other conclusion. *If he is well, why doesn't he come?*

She gave no thought to her own condition. All she knew was that her head hurt and that she was, inexplicably, alone. Shakily, she turned and made her way through the garden towards the house.

It looked empty in the early morning light. There was no sign of anyone stirring and the windows looked blankly across the empty lawn and terrace. Elena stood for a moment, un-certain, trying to decide which was the best door to knock at.

At last, she chose a small door at the far corner, one that looked as if it might lead to the kitchen.

But just as she had made up her mind and was gathering her strength to walk across the lawn to rap at it, she saw it jerk open, and a figure emerged into the bright morning.

It was a Black Priest.

He came out as quietly and quickly as a puff of smoke, and vanished around the corner of the house. The sight of him left Elena weak and shaking. Without a thought she began to circle the house, keeping under cover of the trees. She had no plan at all now, only an urgent sense that she must get away as quickly as she could.

Although the Priest had vanished, Elena could not shake the feeling that he was searching for her. The windows of the house became like eyes, aware of everything she did. She fled into the woods, running blindly among the trees, tripping and scrambling through bushes until, scratched and panting, she came to the high stone wall that surrounded the estate. And there she stopped.

The wall stretched up for fifteen feet without a single finger hold or crevice. Elena turned right and followed the wall, hoping that she could find some means of escape.

She went slowly now, her panic diffused by the sheltering trees. As she went, a fierce resentment burned in her, and she resolved, no matter what happened, that she would not run from the Priests again. She remembered Ariel's words: *These men have no power without your fear.* And at the thought of Ariel, she was filled with such sorrow and rage and loneliness that her throat swelled and tears ran down her cheeks. "But I'm not afraid," she said aloud. "I'm not. I'm not!"

At length she came to the grand gateway through which she and Ariel had entered the evening before. The trees parted a little here, so that it was a pleasant place, dappled with sunlight. Elena summoned all her courage and walked over to the little gatehouse, but there was no sign at all of the gatekeeper. And the gate was securely locked.

Deeply discouraged, Elena crossed to some bushes. "I'll have to wait," she said to herself, and lay down on the thick grass. "I'll watch for him. He'll have to come sometime, and then I'll ask him to let me out. Or maybe I can slip out unnoticed when someone else goes through."

But the events of the night and the morning had left her exhausted, and before she quite realized it, Elena slipped into a deep, dreamless sleep.

She was wakened by a rough shake, the old gatekeeper bending over her.

"Ho, lassie! You can't sleep here."

Elena scrambled to her feet.

"You come along with me," said the keeper.

Elena looked at him warily, keeping a good arm's length between them. "To where?" she said.

"To the house, of course. Come, now."

Elena backed away. "I don't want to go to the house," she said. "I want to go out."

"Nay," said the old man. "There's betters as wants to see you. But the lady said you might be leery. She said to show you this." And he held out something in his hand.

It took Elena a moment to recognize it. A cord of gold, perfectly done up in a knot of Ismay.

18

The Moon, the Rose and a Cup of Tea

"Welcome, my dear," said Lady Fabiad. "And, oh! your poor head! Riddle, bring some warm water and my green case, please. We'll be in the sun room." She led Elena into a brightly lit corner room.

"Now, my dear, sit down on this window seat. Here's a pillow, and don't try to talk."

Dazed, Elena watched silently as Lady Fabiad bustled about bringing towels and a blanket. Shortly there was a tap at the door, and Riddle entered, bearing a large pitcher and a small apple-green wooden box.

"Thank you, Riddle, on the table, please. And if you could ask cook to send up some breakfast for Elena and see that we're not disturbed after that."

"Very good, my lady," said Riddle with a bow, and turned to go.

"Unless," added Lady Fabiad, opening the box, "his lordship or Prince Yadral return. Then let me know immediately."

Riddle turned sharply at this, alarm showing in his eyes. "My lady—" he began.

Lady Fabiad smiled reassuringly and said, "It's all right, Riddle. She is a friend."

Riddle remained unconvinced. "Forgive me, my lady," he said, "but my lord has charged me with guarding the Prince's life. I must ask therefore that this young lady be—"

But here Elena found some semblance of her voice, and croaked, "A—Appin's Will."

Riddle shut his mouth abruptly. With a formal bow in Elena's direction, he turned on his heel and walked out.

"Very good," said Lady Fabiad, laughing. "Very good, my dear. There is more about you than I suspected, though how you learned the password is a mystery to me. I'm sure the Prince didn't give it to you. Now lie back and let me bathe your forehead. When your breakfast comes, we can tell each other stories."

Obediently, Elena lay back in the streaming sunlight and let her hostess minister to her. Lady Fabiad gently washed her wound and then taking some leaves from her green case, made a soothing poultice. "This will help the swelling," she said. Just as she finished binding the poultice in place, there was another tap at the door, and Lou came in, carrying a covered tray.

"Thank you, Lou. Just bring it over here."

As Lou set the tray on a small table, she looked at Elena with evident curiosity. Lady Fabiad explained: "This is Elena, Lou. She entertained us wonderfully last night, but she's had a bump on the head."

"Yes, ma'am," said Lou, "we've met. Are you all right?"

"I think so," said Elena.

"I'm sure my lady will make you better," Lou said, "but if there is anything I can get you, just ask. There's a bell there." She pointed to a corner of the room.

"Well," said Lady Fabiad when Lou had gone, "you must be starving. Let's see what cook has found you on short notice."

Elena gazed at the tray of poached eggs, cheese pie, apple slice, berries and cream, and a large pot of tea. But she had no appetite at all. The Lady Fabiad's kindness, though confusing, had soothed her, and the poultice had eased her head, but she had a concern that went far deeper than hunger.

"What is it, my dear?" asked Lady Fabiad. "Please eat."

"My lady," said Elena, "I—it's Ariel. Do you know where he is?"

"Ah, I *did* think there was something. But I'm sorry, I don't know where he is. I haven't seen him since last night. Perhaps, my dear, I don't like to pry, but perhaps you could tell me all your story, how you came to be where Ismat found you. Then we can try to work this out."

But Elena's story was only too quickly told. She remembered sprinting towards the gardener's cottage after the King had left, and then nothing more until that morning, when she awoke alone, the cottage a shambles, and a sinister trail of blood leading from the door.

"And I was waiting at the gate, to get out, when—Ismat? Is that his name?—found me."

"I see," said Lady Fabiad, frowning. Something in the brief story seemed to puzzle her, but she asked no questions. "Well, I must say I don't like the sound of that blood. But my part of the story is that I knew you were a Daughter, that is, I thought you might be when I first·saw you. And then, after one of your acts, your cord came out, and I saw the knot. This morning, something told me that you might still be around, so I told all the servants to watch for you and bring you to me if they found you. And I was right! But what has happened to Ariel is a mystery. Although," she added, as she poured two cups of tea, "I believe he's all right, and he may well be with Jack or the Prince. Do you feel him anywhere?"

"Feel him?"

"Yes. Don't you feel him anywhere about? I can always tell when Jack's coming home—he's coming home now, as a matter of fact."

"How do you know?" asked Elena, fascinated.

"Well—" Lady Fabiad laughed. "I don't really know how I know, except that I feel different. I feel as if I were with him, even though he's not here. When I feel that way I know he's somewhere about, or will be soon. It's easier, of course, with someone you love.''

Elena considered this for a moment. "Well," she said, "I don't know if this is what you mean, but *I* feel as if something is missing—the way I do when I leave something behind.''

"Hm. Are you worried?''

Elena thought again. "Yes. A little.''

"Are you sad?''

"Sad? . . .No.''

"Then it's probably all right," said Lady Fabiad. "I think he's just gone off somewhere, and will come back as soon as he can. As I said, he's probably with the Prince or Jack. They were haring around in the middle of the night, after the dinner party, and I doubt they even slept. But now, eat some breakfast if you can, and then we'll chat till Jack comes. Maybe he'll have some news about Ariel.''

Thus, in the midmorning sunlight, propped up by pillows, sustained by tea and her first solid food since noon the day before, Elena slowly came to know her new friend, Lady Fabiad.

"But you mustn't call me 'my lady,' " said her hostess. "Just call me Joan, unless there's someone else about that might be offended.''

Very quickly their conversation turned to the Well of Ismay and the Daughters. "Sometimes I thought I was the only one," said Elena. "And I don't know what it *means*.''

Joan laughed. "Nor do I, really. It means you are a certain kind of person though, and any other Daughter I have ever met turned out to be someone I liked immensely and could trust with my life.''

"But what kind of person?" asked Elena. "And what do we do?''

Joan laughed again. "What kind of people are we? It depends. All kinds really. But you will find as you meet other Daughters, that there is *something* in common, something that we share in the heart. And we don't *do* anything."

Elena thought about this, and then said, "He said three things."

"The Three Wisdoms?" said Joan. "Yes. The Moon, The Rose and The Secret Cord."

"I've been turning those over ever since, and I can't make much sense of them."

"I know," said Joan. "It was like that for me, too. But they stay with you, and after a while you build your own meaning into them, if you know what I mean. Now, the moon— well, one quality of the moon is that it's always changing. The sun is the same, day after day, but the moon is in constant change. And we're like that too, changing from minute to minute, really."

Elena nodded, although she was not sure if Joan meant Daughters or everyone.

"Now, the rose, well, roses have thorns. They are so sweet, and their flowers so tender, but they have those sharp thorns for protection. If they didn't have them, they would be picked and trampled by everyone who came along."

"They don't want to be picked," said Elena.

"I think they are glad to be picked," said Joan, "by those who truly love them. Those who are willing to bear the thorns."

Elena said nothing.

"And the secret cord is really just the tie of politeness. Others might feel left out if they knew you were a Daughter of Ismay. It could make for misunderstanding."

There was a long silence while Elena thought about all that Joan had said. A bird called in a distant tree, a liquid stream of song. Joan stirred and exclaimed, "There now! Just as I said."

Before Elena could ask what she meant, the door burst open and Lord Fabiad strode in. His riding clothes were covered in mud, and he looked as though he hadn't slept.

"Hullo," he said, giving Elena a quick nod. "Joan, love, I've brought Ariel back and I want you to see him. He's downstairs in the Flower Room. And I suggest you bring this along," he said, pointing to her green case.

19

Like a Leaf in a Fire

The Flower Room was cool and dark. Elena squinted through the gloom, and then saw Ariel lying on a couch. His eyes were closed, and his face was deathly pale.

"What's wrong with him?" asked Joan, kneeling beside him.

"His leg," said Jack. "Knife wound."

"All right. Bring me blankets, towels and warm water, and have cook send up a pot of bloodroot tea as strong as she can make it."

Over Joan's shoulder, Elena saw the ragged strip of cloth crusted with dried blood, tied above Ariel's left knee.

"Now, Elena," said Joan, "sit here and hold his hand while I see to his leg."

Joan deftly snipped away at Ariel's tights with a pair of scissors. In a moment, she had bared an ugly wound.

"Long," she said, "but not deep. He'll be all right, if it was a clean knife."

Just then Lord Fabiad returned, laden with a large pile of blankets and a stone jug of water.

"Thank you," said Joan, "but you needn't have brought quite so many blankets, and you've forgotten the towels." Riddle came in at that moment, bearing an equally enormous load of towels. "Oh, for heaven's sake," said Joan to Elena, "you would think we had a dozen wounded instead of one! Jack," she went on, "who did this?"

"Black Priest," said Jack tersely.

"Do they put anything on their knives?"

"Poison? I don't think so. At least, not this time. Ariel was over half the countryside with me last night, and it didn't seem to slow him down much."

Joan snorted. "That's what ails him, then. Exhaustion. You should have brought him to me right away, instead of dragging him about in the middle of the night, like a couple of giddy schoolboys."

"We couldn't," said Jack simply. "And most of the time, he was dragging me about."

By this time, Joan had cleaned the wound and begun to dress it with a poultice of the same leaves she had used on Elena's forehead. The clean, slightly sour smell stole through the room. As Elena watched she felt a slight pressure on her hand, and turned to see that Ariel was watching her.

"Hello," he said, in a voice that was little more than a whisper. "Sorry I had to leave you last night." He gave her hand another squeeze.

"How do you feel?"

"Just tired." His eyes took in her bruised forehead. "What happened?"

"I don't know," said Elena. "After the King left, I ran into Moss Alley, and something hit me on the head."

"Aha," said Ariel with a faint laugh. "It was you that saved us! What struck you was a Priest I was chasing. I thought he had tripped on a root."

"Did you catch him?"

"Just. You slowed him just enough. Thank you."

It was Elena's turn to laugh. "I didn't know anything about it," she said. "I didn't come to until morning."

Joan stood up, having finished with the bandage, and said, "You should rest that leg for a couple of days at the very least, Ariel. Let Jack and the Prince be the schoolboys for a while. Now, here's a cup of bloodroot tea. Elena, you make sure he drinks it all. I've got to go and talk to Jack for a minute."

To Elena, the room seemed suddenly large and silent. Unaccountably she found she had nothing at all to say.

"Here, you have to drink this."

Ariel grimaced as he struggled to a sitting position. "Bloodroot tea," he said. "I've been dosed with that before."

"Isn't it very good?"

Ariel took a long swallow, then pulled a hideous face that made Elena laugh. "It's very good," he said, "for the blood. Just what I need, in fact. But it's very bitter."

Elena dipped her finger in the cup and tasted. Her face twisted and Ariel laughed. "But it *is* very good," he said. "And will need to be. I doubt I can arrange to be bed-ridden for as long as Lady Fabiad requires."

"What are we going to do?"

Ariel pursed his lips. "We have to help the Prince," he said. "Although it is such a desperate plan. More desperate than I thought."

"Why?"

"He has very little support and even less real knowledge of what is happening in the Palace."

"What can we do to help?" asked Elena. But before Ariel could reply, the door opened and Prince Yadral himself came in. At the sight of him, Elena scrambled to her feet and stood respectfully beside the couch. Ariel too started to rise, but the Prince, coming forward, bid him be easy.

"I've just come to see how you are," he said to Ariel, "and to meet this young lady, who appears for good or ill to be in the midst of our counsels."

"Certainly, for good," said Ariel. "I am quite well, thank you, thanks to good Lady Fabiad's attentions. Prince Yadral, allow me to introduce Elena, singer, dancer, troubadour, and loyal subject of the King. Elena, Prince Yadral Tha Cneiphon, son of Akheem, Appin bar tailib, crown prince and heir to the throne of Estria.''

''Your highness,'' said Elena, bowing low.

''May fortune follow this meeting,'' replied the Prince formally. ''Though you will forgive me if I say that I would not by choice have involved in our affairs one so young.''

''Good fortune is ever unforeseen,'' said Ariel. ''Elena is young, my lord, but not untested.''

''In this concern, the unforeseen may be our downfall,'' the Prince replied. ''I do not doubt Elena's allegiance to our cause, but our plans are fragile and I have no choice in the matter. I must ask that she remain in this house for the next three days. Perhaps Riddle can find a companion for her, but in any case she must not leave this estate.''

There was a pause, and then Ariel said, ''This is wise policy, my lord, but we may not be able to follow it. You forget that, young though she is, Elena has earned great honour, and through this may prove to be our only hope of success.'' The Prince glanced at Elena, standing silent at the side of Ariel's couch, then looked questioningly at Ariel.

''You forget,'' said Ariel, ''or it may have escaped your notice last night, that Elena was given leave of the Palace Royal and bid before your father the King today at the seventh hour.''

The Prince's mouth tightened. ''All the more reason to keep her here,'' he said. ''That is the last place I would send a child with a secret of arms and apparent insurrection. Until we have cleaned the Palace of the black disease, it is a den of lies and treachery. Both our secret and the girl's life would be like a leaf in a fire.''

''Nevertheless,'' said Ariel patiently, ''I think we must go forward. Consider: after a lapse of many weeks, the King appears suddenly and bestows his trust on a young girl who has won his heart with music. It was no coincidence that he was drawn here where you were, against the wishes of the Priests. It seems they have not conquered his spirit entirely, and we must fight their shadow in any way we can. Innocence and music may be the best weapons we have."

"Then you would hazard all our plans and the kingdom itself on a young girl in a court of intrigue and death?"

"As the King has called her—yes, I would."

The Prince frowned unhappily, and Elena saw the lines between his eyebrows deepen. With his right hand he drummed on a tabletop, and Elena studied his ring—silver, with a blue-green stone carved in the shape of a leaf. At last he said, "I cannot say yes, but I do not say no. In two hours' time we hold council in the Library. I will give my answer then." He turned and walked from the room.

In the silence that followed, Elena felt Ariel grip her hand and give it a reassuring squeeze. Gratefully she squeezed back. She felt very, very hollow.

20

To Answer the Call of the King

"Well, after we had dealt with the priest, which we could not have done without *your* help, my dear, unintentional though it was, the Prince and I had time to meet and introduce ourselves. He was rather suspicious at first. Who wouldn't be, when a stranger turns up knowing his plans, password and all? But I managed to convince him. There, let's stop a moment."

Gently, Ariel sat down on a bench, keeping his wounded leg straight before him. Elena took her place beside him. They were making their way along the south side of the house towards the back, where the Library was. The sunlight lay warm upon them, and from the flower beds around them came the scent of earth, green plants and blossoms and the furry mumble of bees.

After a moment, Ariel continued, "We had a hasty meeting in the dark, the Prince, Lord Fabiad and me, trying to decide what to do. Of course, I had no idea what was going on, really, though it was clear that the coming of the King had upset things quite a bit. We wondered if we shouldn't just confront him, let the Prince talk to him face to face. But it seemed too risky. If we could have gotten him right away from the Priests, it might have worked. As it was, we couldn't be sure where his mind lay. Then Riddle brought word that the King had left and the invasion begun. And for the rest of the night, we were busy putting out fires, so to speak."

"Invasion!" cried Elena. "What invasion?"

"Well," said Ariel, "not a real invasion, and yet it was, in a way. After the King left, a whole boatload of Priests arrived unannounced, and began to slink about the grounds. They were trying, I suppose, to sniff out what it was that had brought the King here. Most of them learned nothing. Two found out," said Ariel with a grim smile, "but they will not be telling. The Prince is not gentle with the Black Priests. At any rate," he continued, "we got them all, and they never reached the house, where there are letters and plans that could be damaging. But come, it's nearly time for the council. Let's walk on."

Elena did not move. She remembered with a chill the Black Priest she had seen leaving the house at dawn. One, it seemed, had escaped the firefighters.

"Ariel," she whispered, "wait . . ."

The Library was a high, light room on the second floor, stuffed to the ceiling with shelves of dusty books. The windows at one end gave a splendid view of the bay, and overhead was a stained glass skylight. In the centre around a wide oak table, sat the Prince, Lord and Lady Fabiad, and Riddle. A clock in a distant hallway struck twelve. Ariel and Elena took their places.

"Before we begin," said the Prince, "I must speak about Elena." He glanced around the table. "Ariel has pointed out that she is bid before my father the King, and so can go where even I cannot just now. This could work to great advantage, but it could work the other way as well. As I bear the responsibility for the lives of many people, and secrecy is of the utmost importance, I have no choice but to forbid this. Forgive me, Elena," he added, looking directly at her. "I mean no disrespect to you."

Ariel cleared his throat in the silence. "My lord," he said, "this secrecy may no longer exist. Elena, tell your story."

Briefly Elena told how that morning she had seen a Black Priest slip out of the house and vanish around the corner.

"Are we to believe this?" the Prince demanded sharply. "Why did you not tell this sooner?"

Elena flushed. "It is true, my lord. I don't know why I didn't tell you—I was confused, perhaps, and then—"

"She had a wicked blow on the head, my lord," cut in Lady Fabiad, "and uninformed as she was, she could not have known the significance to us of such a sight."

Lord Fabiad nodded. "That changes things, anyway. No telling what he found out. Have to alter our plans."

"Unless he found out nothing," said the Prince. "But there is no way of knowing." He grimaced with frustration. "Even if we change our plans and sidestep a counter-attack, they'll be on their guard after this. And we'll have lost our chance."

"My lord, forgive me," said Ariel, "but it now seems more important than ever that Elena be allowed to go to the Palace."

The Prince stared at Ariel in astonishment. "Are you mad? Will you not let this rest? She has nearly brought us to disaster once already. If they know our plans, it would only be throwing her life away."

"No," said Ariel. "If she had not seen what she did and told us, we might now be knotting our own noose. I believe she has brought good fortune, not bad, to your endeavour. I also believe the King's friendship must not be lightly thrown away, especially in a drama where every gesture has meaning. And finally, I believe that she knows so little of your plans as you have disclosed them to me, that if she is found out by the Priests she could reveal nothing. Whereas she might in turn provide invaluable information to us."

"He's right," said Lady Fabiad suddenly. "She should go. It's our only link with the Palace now, and we should use it."

Lord Fabiad looked at his wife, said nothing, but nodded in agreement.

The Prince started to speak, then stopped. He pursed his lips, drummed his fingers on the table top and stared hard at Elena, as though looking inside her. At last, after a long silence, he said simply, "So be it."

With a rush and a clatter, the carriage swept out through the great stone gateway. Inside rode Joan Fabiad and a very nervous Elena. "I'll drop you off near the Palace," Joan was saying. "Remember, pretend that you are a silly girl, overawed by the King's attention. You'll be much safer to go disguised as a giggling fool." Elena wondered how she could raise even the ghost of a giggle under the circumstances.

Before they had climbed into the green and gold carriage, Ariel had taken Elena's hand and drawn her aside under a flowering tree.

"Do you know what you are doing?" he asked her.

"No," she said, simply.

"You are going into a very dangerous place," he said, "but you go there with the friendship of the King, to sing and dance and play for him. His heart has been deeply wounded by these Priests. They have played upon his fears, confused him and abused his trust. More than anything now, he needs an honest friend, and I think that may be you."

Ariel paused for a moment, and looked up into the flowering canopy above them. "Don't try too hard to steal the secrets of the Priests. They are so suspicious and wary that innocence and an open heart are your only hope. Always be alert, and remember that something that means nothing to you may be filled with meaning for the Prince."

He paused again and shifted his leg, almost unconsciously. He bowed his head and he seemed to listen intently for a moment. Then he looked into Elena's eyes. "This is your task.

I would not have chosen it for you. But remember that the Brotherhood is with you wherever you go, although it may not be present in form. Ask for help not for yourself but for others, and you will be answered. Be above fear, Elena. And remember. Remember this.''

As the carriage sped down the avenues of the High Hills, Elena felt that still moment within her, an anchor against the storms of nervous energy that now swept through her. Although she had no idea what Ariel meant in saying, ''Remember this,'' the light of his glance was still burning in her heart.

21

Into the Palace

Elena stood at the edge of the broad greystone square, and looked across it to the main palace gate. Shops and flower stalls edged the square, and women of the quarter hurried to and fro with baskets on their arms, intent on their daily marketing. Beyond them, stretching up tower upon tower, a mountain of fretted stone, stood the Palace itself.

How strange, thought Elena, *that they can go calmly about their business practically in the shadow of the Palace*. She moistened her lips and swallowed. Here she was at the edge of the square, facing her destination: the Palace of the King, in Rakhbad, the City of the King. The centre of all Estria.

It seemed to take an age to cross the square. Closer and closer she walked to the great walls and towers, with their forbidding arrowslits and battlements, and the massive iron gate. The Palace was a fortress, built in days gone by when the King often had to defend his throne in battle. If Elena had known where to look, she would have seen the grim marks of fire and bloodshed upon it still.

At last she came to the broad gateway. Two enormous soldiers with long black beards stood guard there, one on each side of the gate. They stood impassively, massive arms folded on their chests and long naked swords stuck in their belts. Neither moved a muscle as Elena approached.

She looked up at one and said, "Excuse me, I—I've come

to see the King." She felt so silly saying this though, that she was not surprised when the black giant merely growled, "Get on with you! Do you think the King is a sideshow?"

But she could not let herself be turned away. "No, sir," she said. "But the King has asked me to come. My name is Elena, and the King has given me leave of the Palace."

The guard glanced at her contemptuously and said, "What do you know about leave of the Palace? Go play your games somewhere else before I paddle you!"

"I hardly believe it myself," said Elena, "but in truth the King has bid me come at the seventh hour and given me leave of the Palace. It was just last night he did so. Perhaps he hasn't told you?"

The guard stared at her for a long moment, and when she neither flinched nor turned away, he growled, "If this is a tale, you're in for a thrashing, that's for sure. Arban!" he shouted to the other guard. "One to Watch!" And then he disappeared through a side door.

The minutes dragged by as Elena waited, standing at the foot of one great tower. Although she was still in the open square, she felt as though the gates had already clanged to behind her. This was largely because of the implacable stare of the other guard, whose concentration upon her never wavered throughout a long quarter of an hour. At last the first guard returned, and without a word beckoned her through the side door.

She followed the guard down a short hallway, to a small stone cell of a room that seemed to be an office. Again without a word, the guard turned and left her.

Behind a battered stone slab that served as a desk a small, grey-faced man sat, in the midst of his dinner. He had shrewd, unfriendly eyes, and his wide, sneering mouth was still greasy from his meal.

"Well," he said, "what are you bothering the guards for?"

100

He waited, as though expecting an explanation, but when Elena started to speak, he went on, "We get this all the time, little girls and boys with silly ideas, simply wasting our time, trying to fool us, thinking we haven't seen their childish games a hundred times before." Suddenly he banged his hand on the slab and shouted, "I could throw you in the dungeon, do you know that? And nobody would know you were there!"

But Elena was undaunted. Unlike the guard, this man inspired no fear in her at all. She suddenly heard herself saying, as steady as steel, "I have been given leave of the Palace by his majesty King Akheem, and I am bid before him at the seventh hour. The time grows short. Will you delay me?"

At these words the man checked himself, and Elena saw fear flicker in his eyes. Then he blustered, "All right, all right, if that's how you want it, we'll just send you to Mizrab, he knows how to deal with little girls like you! Guard! Guard!" And in a moment, she was led away from the stone cell, down more corridors and passageways, ever deeper into the Palace.

The guard, every bit as large and ferocious as the first, led her at last to a small common room where half a dozen officers were eating, drinking and gambling around a rough table. The guard thrust Elena through the open doorway, shouted "One for Mizrab!" and left without further explanation. There was a muttered oath from one with his back to her.

"Hold your throw, Harbab," he growled as he stood up. "I've got fifty bits riding on this. I want to see those bones roll with my own eyes." Then he turned and saw Elena.

"By the horns! What's this? How did your young ladyship come here?"

"I am Elena. I was given leave of the Palace by his majesty the King, and bid appear before him at the seventh hour. Your guards have hindered me."

There was a murmur from around the table, and a voice said, "Probably Misha. Head like a turnip, that one." "Bangor," said another. "I saw him bring her in." And Mizrab said, "A misunderstanding, my lady. I shall speak to the guard myself. Here, Brother," he said, clapping one of the others on the shoulder, "I'm bound here till the watch changes. Will you take her ladyship to the Warden of the Chambers?"

Wordlessly, the soldier got up. Since Elena had first spoken, he had been watching her closely. Now, with a curious look and a short bow, he led her from the room. When they were out of earshot of the others he fell into step beside her and said softly, "How is our Brother Ariel?"

Elena felt her stomach lurch and her skin crawl, but she managed to control her face and keep walking as though she hadn't heard. In the silence there was only their footsteps and the violent hammering of her heart.

Then the soldier spoke again. "Hadrat, Sergeant of the King's Patrol. Two days' journey down from Ballafan, two weeks ago. But you were no lady then."

Elena cast a quick look sideways, but still she said nothing. They passed a deep doorway where a soldier stood motionless on guard, and Hadrat saluted without breaking stride. The soldier woodenly returned the salute.

"Chamber of the Exchequer," he said, when they were past. "When there *is* an Exchequer. Don't worry, I'll keep your mouse wrapped up, whatever it is. Tell Ariel the fifth patrol is loyal." And suddenly he quickened his pace and led her round a corner and into a panelled and carpeted chamber.

"A lady for the Warden of the Chambers!" he barked. "Leave of the Palace Royal!"

An old man, clad in thick purple robes with a gold chain and seal about his neck, had been dozing over a desk. At the sound of voices he suddenly sat up and blurted, "—and all the Lord Mayors of the Realm! Use the second seal, not the—what? Where is that boy?" A scribe's stool stood by him, with ink, pen and paper to hand, but the old man was alone in the chamber.

"A lady," said Hadrat, standing at attention before him. "Given leave of the Palace Royal and bid appear before the King at the seventh hour."

"Given leave!" said the old man in astonishment. "Appear before the King? Most extraordinary! What is your name, my dear?"

Elena bowed. "I am Elena," she said.

"Of . . .?" said the old man, and Elena replied levelly, "Of Estria."

"Ah, hmm, I see. Untitled," said the old man, and shuffled absently through some papers on his desk. "I don't seem to . . . Leave Royal, you say? . . . I don't have any . . ."

"His Majesty did me this honour last night," said Elena. "He made a brief—" She stopped in mid-sentence, feeling a cold breath of air steal over her. With it came a strange reluctance to say any more about the King. Turning, she saw a Priest standing silently in the corner, where none had been before.

"Pray, continue," he said, bowing sardonically. When Elena remained silent, he glanced coldly at Hadrat and said, "Thank you, Sergeant. You may go."

As Hadrat's steps died away, the Priest glanced at the old man. "The King is wearied from his studies," he said. "We have arranged this—entertainment." He said it with a sneer. "Come." He held aside a curtain. "This way."

She followed him down a dark and endless stairway until at last they came to a large, brass-bound door. There, the Priest halted. "Come here."

Unwillingly, Elena stepped forward, one pace, two, until she could feel the Priest's breath on her forehead and his malevolent gaze drilling into her.

"Listen to me," he said, a hand like cold iron gripping her arm. "We know what you are. Your tricks are useless here. Do you understand? Useless! The King is ours!" And he shook her once, very hard.

Then he opened the door.

22

Madness in the Tower

Elena was at one end of a wide low-ceilinged hall, pillared, beamed and floored all with blood-red stone that dully gleamed in the flickering of torches set into the walls. There was a reek in the air that caught in the back of her throat and made her gag. From nowhere in particular a high-pitched, monotonous chanting echoed through the hall.

By the light of the torches Elena could make out statues of ancient kings and queens ranged along the walls, seated on thrones carved from the same blood-red stone. Glistening in the torchlight, they seemed to be alive.

The Priest had disappeared. Uncertainly, Elena took a step forward, and another, and then another. It was not until she was perhaps a third of the way down the hall that she placed the source of the strange droning sound. The last two niches along the left-hand side had no statues in them. In the last but one a Priest sat before a low brazier, monotonously plucking a single-corded drone and keening a chant into the fluttering blue flames.

Elena paused there for a long time but the Priest seemed unaware of her. His face was haggard and he crouched forward, almost leaning into the fire. His hand raggedly thrummed the drone and his eyes were glazed and unseeing, as though he had been chanting thus for many hours. As Elena stood there, she caught herself slipping into the hold of the endless sound, and with an effort pulled her gaze away from the Priest. Only then did she become aware of the eyes of the King watching her from the darkness at the end of the hall.

He was slumped in a large chair, set as though it were a throne in a throne room. He was as grey and motionless as death in the wavering semi-darkness. Only his eyes were alive, burning dully, as with a fever.

Elena went forward and dropped to one knee, bowing her head. "My lord King, I am come at your bidding."

The King stirred slightly and said, "Has it worked? Are you the first of my new subjects? What little queen are you?" His faint voice barely rose above the chanting of the Priest.

"I am no queen, my lord, though I am your subject. I am Elena."

"You . . . Elena? No queen was ever . . . called Elena . . ." The King cleared his throat. It was a faint, distant sound, like dry leaves being slipped from hand to hand. "When did you live? Are you from the ancient past, before the lists were written?"

"Forgive me, my lord," said Elena. "I do not understand. Last night in Lord Fabiad's garden . . ."

The King stirred again, and his eyes flickered.

" . . . I sang and danced for you. My lord did me the great honour of granting me leave of the Palace Royal and bidding me appear before you at the seventh hour."

The King gazed at Elena as though seeing her for the first time. "Is it the seventh hour now?" he asked.

"A little past, perhaps, my lord. I came as quickly as I could."

"The seventh hour . . ." The King's gaze wandered across the hall and fell upon the Priest, still chanting in his niche. A shadow crossed his face. Then he slowly turned back to Elena, standing patiently before him.

"What is your name?"

"Elena, my lord."

"Elena? You are a . . . singer?"

"Yes, my lord."

"They did not want you to come. I made them let you. I told them last night if they kept you out, I would keep them out. Did they hurt you?"

"No, my lord."

"It is dark in here. Have they draped the windows?"

Elena looked about her, then said, "Windows there are none, my lord." She remembered what Ariel had told her. "I think this is the Red Chamber."

"The Red Chamber?" The King stared about again. "The Red Chamber. Yes, it is." Suddenly he stood up. "Come," he ordered, and strode away into the shadows.

When Elena caught up to him, he was standing by a curtain. "Shhh," he said, putting a finger to his lips. "They don't know about this. They nose everything out, and they think they know everything, but they don't know this door! Only the King!" He glanced furtively around before leading the way behind the dusty curtain. There he unlocked a small door. "Quick!" he hissed. "In here!"

The door shut behind them, leaving them in total darkness. Beside her, Elena heard a dry, rasping sound: the laughter of the King. "Come," he said. Finding her hand in the dark he led her up a stairway.

After a very long climb, the stairwell went from black to grey. Light filtered down from above, and Elena could now make out the stone steps before her and the form of the King beside her. He seemed to be in a most unusual state of mind, and from time to time would mutter to himself or laugh almost soundlessly.

At last, holding hands and puffing, they came to the top of the stairs. Above them a tall, arched window caught what must have been the last light of the setting sun. A band of pink and gold fell on the stone wall opposite. What they could see of the sky was deep blue and cloudless.

"Shhh, hush," said the King, drawing forth a ring of keys. "They don't know. They don't know. We must be quiet as mice." With elaborate care, he slid a key into the lock, slowly and silently turned it, and pulled the door ajar. Gesturing for Elena to wait, he slipped through and disappeared. He was back immediately, and led her down a short hallway to another heavy curtain. At this he paused, listened, and when he was satisfied, cautiously peeked through. Then, in a last silent rush, he hurried her across a broad open hall into a small room. He pulled the door to and barred it.

The bare room had two tall windows with a stone writing easel set between them. Below the easel was an ancient brass and leather trunk. Through the windows, Elena looked west high over the Palace. To her left lay the still waters of the bay; before her the fiery red globe of the sun was just sinking out of sight behind the High Hills.

The King sat down, propping himself against the wall. He threw his head back, closed his eyes, and breathed noisily through his mouth. The last bit of daylight lent his face colour it had not had in the depths of the Red Chamber, but it also revealed the extent of his ordeal there. Lined, unshaven, haggard, it seemed more like the face of a weary peasant than that of a King. Or, Elena thought, like the faces of the two men in the cart at Ballafan, the exiles fleeing for their lives.

The King sat for so long without moving that Elena began to think he had fallen asleep. Suddenly he opened his eyes and said, "Did you eat?"

"My lord?"

"The evening meal. Did you eat the evening meal yet?"

"N-no, my lord, I did not," Elena answered.

"I will bring it. Wait here." Abruptly he stood and was gone.

For a long time Elena watched out the window as night fell over Rakhbad. When it was quite dark, she heard a noise behind her, and turned to see the King throw down a sack in the middle of the room. He was breathing heavily and his eyes were shining. "Almost," he said. "Almost . . . They . . . never! Ha! I . . . never!" And he slumped down on the floor in the same place as before. "Food," he said, gesturing towards the sack. "The King's Table." And without another word he rolled over and fell asleep.

After a few moments Elena dragged the sack over to a window and in the faint light, untied it. She found a strange assortment of things inside, but not a great deal of food. There were several tablecloths, three fine china plates and a handful of golden butter-knives, as well as an enormous candelabra (but no means to light it), some crusts of bread, an onion and a bottle of sweet cider.

Well, she thought, *the King's Table. Not fine or full, but served by the King himself.* Philosophically, she set to. She had eaten many a poorer meal, and been glad of it, when on the road with Ariel.

After half the meagre rations were gone, she brushed the crumbs from her lap and began to consider what to do. *I could go out*, she thought, *into the rest of the Palace. But what would I do there? Find Hadrat. But I don't want to run into a Priest, even if I have been given the leave of the Palace.*

She peered at the sleeping form of the King. He had not moved since lying down. *I suppose "leave" means I can come and go as I want, but I don't think the King wants me to go from here tonight. And I don't think he should be alone, either. He seems very unhappy.*

The room was growing cool, and the court dress she wore was thin, so Elena sat down by the sleeping King and drew the heavy linen tablecloths over them both like blankets. Soon,

109

with the gathering warmth and the weariness of the long day, Elena lay down and fell asleep.

She awoke in the middle of the night. The King stood by one window, gesturing feverishly. His gestures were strange, but he seemed to be in the midst of some struggle, with whom or what Elena could not tell. Again and again he flung up his arms, thrusting, pulling, signalling frantically, all in eerie silence, except for the flapping of his clothes and the occasional suppressed groan. As she watched, his gestures became more frantic, the pace more and more agitated, until at last, with a sudden cry of "No! No! My son!" he collapsed exhausted to the floor.

Elena crawled over to him, but already he was once again in a deep sleep. She wondered if he had been asleep all along. Gathering the tablecloths once more, she lay down beside the King, and tucked them both in.

But she did not sleep again for a long while. The moon had appeared in one corner of the tall window. Watching it riding and shining in the night, Elena thought of Joan Fabiad. The Wisdom of the Moon and the memory of Joan were very comforting to her just then, for she knew, with absolute certainty, that the King of Estria was mad.

23

Life Wagered for Life

When Elena awoke in the morning she was alone. Sitting up, stiff and sore from her night's sleep on the cold stone floor, she saw the door to the chamber wide open and the King gone. Across the bay, the first rays of the sun were brushing the trees on the High Hills.

Elena stretched and groaned. She felt bruised in mind and body. Her head ached with a dull steady throb that quickened with every sudden movement. Her fine court dress was hopelessly crumpled.

She cautiously stood and considered her situation. *I'm not much of a fine lady*, she thought, *even if I did sleep in the Palace*. Around her were strewn the remains of the "King's Table" from the night before, including the tablecloths she and the King had slept in. There was still some cider in the bottle, and she drank it gratefully.

I should try to find the King, she decided. *He's my only friend here, really, and he shouldn't be alone. I hope he hasn't gone far.* But before she left the chamber, she gathered everything up in the sack and stowed it behind the door. *No point in telling more than we need. If they don't know where we are, so much the better.* Then she stepped carefully through the doorway.

She was in a high empty hall, obviously at the top of a tower, for at either end, stone steps led downward. Across the hall was the curtained doorway through which they had come the evening before. Through an eastern window high up in the wall, there poured a stream of sunlight, splashing the deserted hall and making it seem quite peaceful.

Where would he go? Elena walked slowly to the balustrade at one end and looked down, but the flight of stairs was all she could see. The tower seemed unused, for though she listened a long time no sound at all came up to her.

There's no point in going back to the secret stair. It will be dark, and it only seems to lead to the Red Chamber. I don't want to go there again. So I suppose I shall have to go down these stairs.

She was just about to descend when a shadow moved across the shaft of sunlight. Looking up, Elena was astonished to see the King standing outside the eastern window, his arms raised as if in invocation.

"Well," said Elena, "easier than I thought to find him. But how do I get up to him? And what on earth is he doing?"

For the King remained frozen, with his arms raised, facing the sun.

The top of the tower was plain and bare, but it took Elena many minutes of searching before she found the way to the King. Behind the curtained doorway, another curtain concealed another staircase. Elena might not have found it at all, had she not noticed a worn spot on the embroidery of the heavy. cloth. "But I should have expected it," she muttered to herself as she hurried up the stairs. "Hidden stairs everywhere you look, it seems. It's a wonder the walls can stand up at all."

She stepped out onto a narrow walkway bordered by a waist-high parapet. There was a vast and giddy view of the bay, and far below, the roofs and courtyards of the Palace, but Elena did not stop to look.

Quickly, she went to the corner and looked around. The

King was there kneeling against the parapet, chin resting on his folded arms.

"Hello," he said mildly, as she stepped into view. "Good morning."

"Good morning, your Majesty. All peace be yours."

The King gravely inclined his head. "Thank you. But there is the true majesty. The Real King." He pointed to the sun, rising in the fresh blue sky. It shone on the city with a startling vividness and on the harbour and the eastern plains.

Elena looked carefully at the King's face. In the bright light, she could clearly see the marks of struggle—a struggle with madness and the mad schemes of the Priests. But the night's sleep in the tower had rested him. Fear and worry seemed to have lifted a little, leaving his face lined only with sorrow. He gestured for her to sit down beside him.

"My lord," said Elena, "I—"

But he silenced her and turned once more towards the sun. For a long time he knelt so, his eyes closed and his face lifted into the sunlight, almost as if he were breathing it in. At last, without turning, he said, "That is a power they know nothing of."

"My lord?"

"The sun. The Priests know nothing of the sun. They deny it."

There was another silence. Elena said, "My lord, what is it that they seek to do?"

The King turned and with an expression Elena could not fathom, said, "They claim to offer me another kingdom. One which will never perish. Where the subjects serve forever."

"Another kingdom . . . ?"

The King's eyes grew cold. "More lasting than the Kingdom of Estria, where there is deceit and treachery and lies, where sons betray their fathers and trusted friends prove false. The Priests would give me mastery of the Kingdom of the Dead."

As he finished speaking, Elena saw once more a touch of madness in his face. "Do you believe it, my lord?" she asked. "Can this be done?"

The King stared at her and then turned away. "I must believe," he said. "I must. They have shown there is nothing else. They have shown me nothing can be trusted. Swords can rust and splinter. Friends can turn away. My son—" He broke off, his mouth working, and stared across the city.

Elena could think of nothing to say. After a moment, the King continued.

"I have wanted to resist them. When I was a boy, my father brought me here each morning to pray. We prayed in the sunlight for peace, health and prosperity to spread upon this land. Each morning we climbed the stairs and knelt here praying, no matter what the weather, because my father said the sun was there, shining, if we could see it or not.

"But the Priests have made all dark. One by one, they have broken the lamps of my life. Would to God they had been wrong! Each time they have been right has been like bitter ashes in my mouth."

"My lord, your son the Prince—"

"That was the worst." The King turned his eyes upon her, and Elena saw pain and anger mixed with weariness and age. "You are young. You have not felt how a parent grows through a child; how the parent lies beneath the soil like a root, feeding and sustaining the child, that he may grow and flower and bear fruit."

The King paused. "A week ago, my son came to the Palace and unannounced visited the servants' quarters. He left with a scullery maid, with whom he was apparently infatuated. Together they climbed up to this tower, and after writing me a snivelling note of apology, they threw themselves off.

"I found them myself," he added, "since they fell into my private courtyard. I could only recognize my son by his shoes."

The King turned away then, and for a long time he and Elena sat in silence. The tale of the Prince's death struck Elena like a blow. She felt sickened by the treachery of the Priests, and the needless pain and despair of the King.

"My lord King," she ventured at last, "could this not have been a . . . deception? Part of a plot?"

"Do you think I wish to believe this cowardice? The letter was in his hand; there was that in it that no one else could know."

"B—but my lord," stammered Elena, "I—I have seen him!"

"What?" The King whirled around and Elena saw a spark of hope kindle in his eyes. "Where?"

"In . . . in the city, my lord. Only yesterday. He asked me not to say just where, for fear of the Priests. He distrusts them, my lord, but he is loyal to you as any loving son would be."

The King stared at her for a long moment, hope and dread of disappointment wavering on his face. At last he said, "If this is false, you know your life is forfeit? To play so upon the feelings of a father would be too cruel for you to hope for any mercy."

But Elena was undaunted. "My lord, he will show himself alive within three days. I know it."

"Will he? Will he?" And suddenly, as though accepting a challenge, the King pulled himself upright and fixed her with a keen glance. "Very well. You have three days of life at least. If he comes within that time, good fortune is yours for the rest of your life. But if my son the Prince does not appear, you die by fire on the morning of the fourth day. So be it!"

And Elena, dry-mouthed, could only reply, "The King's will be done."

24

The Fury of the Priest

Not long after, the King and Elena descended the tower into the rest of the Palace. Elena had expected to find all in an uproar because the King had disappeared. She had forgotten that, for most of the Palace, the King had disappeared long ago, and that the various nobles and functionaries had begun to live as though there were no King at all.

It was a considerable shock, therefore, for the three guards lolling on the dais of the Throne Room consuming a late and messy breakfast, to find the King himself suddenly standing before them, looking bleak and wintery indeed.

"Your Majesty!" they cried, leaping to their feet amid a shower of crumbs and chicken bones.

"You," growled the King, pointing to one whose mouth still bulged with food, "out and bring your captain here, and do it double quick. On your life!"

With a muffled, "Y'f, y'r Mj'fty!" he fled from the hall, while the others stood frozen. "I'm surprised you didn't find the throne more comfortable," the King said, after he had looked them thoroughly up and down, whereupon they both flushed scarlet.

Elena surveyed the Throne Room. It was altogether different from the Red Chamber. To call it a room seemed inappropriate, for it was as broad and long as a good-sized field, under an immense vaulted ceiling. The stonework was milk white, veined with the palest shades of blue, drenched now with light from the tall windows. Inlaid in the floor was a mosaic of a green and graceful tree, its roots towards the great audience doors, and its spreading branches toward the throne.

It was clear, though, that the room had been neglected for many days. The audience doors were shut, the chairs and tables down the sides of the great room were in disarray. Elena saw a goblet lying forgotten beside an overturned stool.

The sound of running feet announced the return of the guard, followed closely by his captain and two white-faced stewards. Each bobbed a quick bow as he came through the door, and then hastened across the floor towards the waiting King. The Captain was about to speak when the King waved him into silence, and pointed at the dais.

"Look," he commanded. "Is this how you fulfill your command?"

The Captain looked and turned pale. "Your Majesty—" he began.

"You have done poorly," said the King, cutting him off. "You are relieved of your post. Clean this up, and then get out of the Palace. You three, go to Prabst in the stables. If he doesn't need three idiots for mucking out, you can be gone as well. And you two," he said, swinging upon the open-mouthed stewards, "jump to your business! I will hold audience here at the third hour. Have the heralds proclaim it."

And then, ignoring them all, he mounted the dais and took his place upon the throne. He sat there for a long moment, staring down towards the great doors, and then turned to Elena. "A stool," he said. "Here. And sing."

And so Elena brought a stool and placed it where he showed her, a little to one side on the broad dais, and sat and after a minute, began to sing.

When she was done, there was a Black Priest standing before

the dais. He wore a sarcastic smile and was looking,. Elena felt, not at the King, but at her.

"King of Kings," he said. "King of Both Worlds." And he bowed slowly and deeply.

Elena found it difficult to look away from the Priest. There was something powerful and compelling about his eyes, and something horribly fascinating about the two white scars on his left cheekbone: two white points, like the bite of a snake.

"Chashra," replied the King. "Priest."

The Priest inclined his head at thus being named, and said. "Your Majesty seeks amusement in the false kingdom. It is good."

"I am glad it meets with your approval," replied the King drily. For a moment, Elena thought she could see anger flicker in the Priest's cold eyes, but he replied with another smooth bow, and said, "Your Majesty has been labouring long to claim your proper Kingdom. A little amusement before the final battle shows the true wisdom of a King."

The King made no response at all.

"And what a quaint and unexpected companion," Chashra continued. "A beggar girl, to sit beside the Throne of the Two Worlds, singing her childish songs. A novel fancy, my lord." And the Priest's lips curled in a mirthless smile. "But my lord, I pray you, do not let this moment's play delay you from the ceremony. Today at the third hour there is the Ceremony of Passing Over, in the Red Chamber. It is most important that you be there."

"Indeed?" said the King. "I will *not* be there. I will hold audience at the third hour."

"In the Red Chamber, my lord?"

"Here, Chashra. In the Throne Room of Estria."

"The Throne Room of Estria." The Priest repeated the words as though they meant "The Doll's House" or "The

Stable Yard." "My lord, there are subjects who await you in a far greater kingdom than Estria." His faded grey eyes fixed implacably on the King. "It is the greatest land, my lord King, for all must come there. Friends and enemies alike will live there under your dominion. And of course . . . loved ones," he added with a lingering sneer. "The Rites have been prepared, my lord King. All is ready. Will you throw away this single chance for an afternoon of idle play?"

The King sat unmoving. At last he said, "Why do you trouble me?"

The Priest's voice dropped to a croon. "It is this world which troubles you, O King. We only seek to lift your burden. Come to the Red Chamber at the third hour, and with the Ceremony of Passing Over we will invest you as a True King, and give you the son you deserve."

The King seemed about to respond, but before he could, Elena jumped to her feet, and in a clear voice, said, "Your Majesty!" There was a sharp hiss from the Priest. The King turned and said, "Yes?"

Elena had no clear idea what she was doing.

Recklessly, she said, "My lord, I beg you leave to ask Priest Chashra a question."

"What would you ask, daughter?"

"I would ask, my lord—I would ask—" she floundered. Suddenly, unlooked-for strength welled up in her. She heard herself say, "I would ask him why he hides the face of the True King?"

The Priest's mouth contorted and he went white with rage, spitting out, "Beggar girl! Witch! Begone!"

The King turned impassively to him. "Priest, can you answer this?"

Shaking with anger, the Priest drew himself up and said, "I will not be questioned by a witch-girl, my lord. Beware! She is treachery itself, filled with spells and lies and evil. She will lead you astray! But my lord," the Priest stepped nearer and lowered his voice, "if you wish to see your loved one again, you will come to the Red Chamber at three. Long life and health," he added with a snarl, and strode from the Throne Room.

The King and Elena remained still for a long time. Finally the King stirred and called out, "Steward!" Instantly a boy appeared, and the King said, "Send a message to the Priests in the Red Chamber. Tell them to wait three days. On the fourth day, perhaps, they shall have their rite. And steward, see that the Lady Elena be given what she needs. She will be a guest of the Palace for at least three days. But on no account may she leave the grounds. He who allows her to go shall die."

25

The Warning of the Scorpion

Ibby, the steward, treated Elena with great respect, asked no questions and served her promptly. He brought her to a ground-floor room in the West Wing. Its windows were shaded by a beautiful weeping birch tree, and beyond, Elena could glimpse the corner of a flower garden.

Ibby brought a wardrobe of court clothes, which surprisingly fit Elena quite well, and a great jug of hot water, soap and towels. Lastly, and most welcome of all, he brought food: a tray loaded with soup and bread, poached fish and carrot buskins, tea and lemon wafers and fruit. Then, discreetly, he withdrew.

Elena was starved. She fell upon the food and ate steadily. Only when she was on her second cup of tea and her fifth lemon wafer did she begin to consider her situation.

So I'm Lady Elena now, she thought. *But it might be a rather short stay among the gentry. I wish I knew more about the Prince's plans. He said three days, but maybe he's changed his mind, and then wouldn't I be in a fine fix . . . If only I knew some way of sending a message out . . . not just for me. The King seems more—awake, somehow, but if those Priests ever get him into their ceremony, whatever it is, I think he'll be asleep for good.*

She crossed to the open window. Through the fine, graceful branches of the birch tree, she could feel the heat of the gathering day. *I know Sergeant Hadrat. I think I could trust him . . . if I knew what I wanted to do . . .*

But then it struck her that she could send a message to Ariel at the inn without drawing attention to the wrong quarter. Surely it would reach him. She pulled the heavy bell-cord and in a moment Ibby appeared, bowing in the doorway.

"How might I speak with Hadrat, Sergeant of the fifth patrol?"

Ibby's face revealed nothing as he replied, "Alas, my lady, it cannot be done. The fifth patrol left this morning to manoeuvre in the Northeast Duchy. They will be gone at least a week."

"Oh," said Elena. "I see. Thank you."

Eventually she went outside and wandered dispiritedly through the gardens. They were broad and majestic in their layout. Almost every turn revealed a new view—an ancient tree, a fountain, or the bay. But somehow, there was an air of neglect that made Elena feel she was the first to have walked there for days. The flowerbeds were untended, and the walkways littered with leaves. She met no one, neither gentlefolk nor gardeners.

At length she came through a narrow wicket gate into another part of the grounds and her nose caught the smell of horses. Her heart gave a leap. *It must be the stables! And Ariel has a friend here. What was his name?* Desperately she searched her memory for the sunlit afternoon she had spent with Ariel atop the abandoned tower and felt the name brush tantalizingly past her. . . . *Liander! It was Liander!*

She started eagerly towards the long sheds before her, but then stopped, considering. *Ariel wouldn't say if Liander was in the Brotherhood or not,* she mused. *He called him a friend, but that may not mean much. If I give him a message for Ariel, who knows where it will end up? But I haven't much to work with just now. I shall just have to be careful, and see what I can see.* And resolutely, she started again towards the stables.

She turned into a kind of alleyway between two long stables. In the darkness under the overhanging eaves, she could make out stall after stall, but most of them were empty.

She was uncomfortably aware of the oddness of her situation. She was not dressed for the stables, but rather as a lady of the Palace, and she had no idea if the fine women of the court ever went near the horse barns. Self-consciously she plucked up her skirts and went on. She felt as though someone were watching her, although she had not seen a single person. The stables had the same deserted air as the gardens.

Coming suddenly upon a side alley, she nearly tripped over a small groom leading an enormous black stallion. The horse started and reared, almost trampling the groom under its hooves. Elena jumped out of the way and stood apprehensively against the stable wall while the groom fought to control the animal.

"Now, lady, that was a start, and no mistake," he said, turning to her at last. "Powder can't be trusted without a rider, you see. With an officer on his back, he's steady as steel, but otherwise, he frights easy."

"I'm sorry," said Elena, flushing.

"No harm done," said the groom, "and no blame. How was you to know we'd be coming up just then?"

The groom was tiny, about the same size as Elena, with quick eyes and a husky voice. He looked open and engaging, and if he was surprised to find a lady such as Elena about the stable, he certainly did not show it. "Amhash, at your service," he said, and touched his cap with his free hand.

"Elena at yours," said Elena and dropped a curtsey. "I'm looking for a man named Liander."

"Liander!" said the groom. "Do you know him?"

"No," said Elena "A f—friend asked me to—to see him."

"Certainly, lady. Down there. Can't miss him." And he

nodded down the side alley from which he had come. He did not move, though, and Elena found the way uncomfortably narrowed by the presence of Powder.

"It's all right," the groom told her as she sidled gingerly past. "He's steady now. He knows you're about." *No doubt*, thought Elena. *And I wonder who else now knows I'm about. What am I getting myself into?*

Then she noticed the sound of a small smithy. A dapple grey mare stood quietly there, meditating solemnly on a nosebag of oats, but Elena couldn't see anyone nearby. Then she caught a movement in the darkness behind the horse, and walking round, found the blacksmith at work on one of the mare's hind hoofs.

He was a sturdy man, with humped shoulders and arms like casks, broad hands and fingers like sausages. Elena stood quietly and was astonished at the gentleness and delicacy of his huge hands as he carefully pared the hoof. She was convinced that, Brother or not, if this was Liander she could trust him.

At last he finished and straightened up. Elena stepped forward and said, "Liander?"

The blacksmith turned to her, his face lit up with a broad grin, revealing half a dozen widely spaced rotten teeth.

"Liander," she went on, "I am Elena. I—I'm a friend of Ariel's." The grin remained, the great head nodded encouragingly, but Elena saw no light of comprehension in the eyes.

"Ariel," she repeated. "You know, the—the juggler. We are friends. I wanted to ask you to—"

"It's no good," the groom's voice cut in from behind her. "No use at all. He's deaf as a stone, that one. Has been all his life. Only creatures he understands is horses." But Liander did not see the groom. He had his gaze fixed upon Elena, and grinned and nodded like a long lost friend, and Elena felt her heart would break with every nod.

When she returned to her room in the Palace, it was evening. She was deeply discouraged, but her spirits rose when she saw that the steward had been there. A lamp was lit, her bed had been turned down and a covered tray on the table promised food.

Elena was hot and tired, and she wanted to wash before she ate. She stopped short, however, when she saw the nightrobe hanging on the bathroom door. The heavy belt was twisted in a scorpion knot, the Parsat sign for mortal danger.

Quickly she scanned the bathroom for signs of another message, but there were none. She touched the knot, gingerly, as though it might be a real scorpion. Who put this here? she thought. Could it be Ibby? The robe swung gently under her hand.

Then she heard footsteps in the corridor. Almost immediately, she was skinning noiselessly out the window. She pushed it shut behind her and sank into the shadows, and heard a heavy knock on the door. In a moment it was repeated, and then the door swung open and two figures stepped inside.

They were Priests. Elena caught the gleam of metal in their hands, but before they could cross the room she was gone, running through the night.

26

Death Follows After

Elena spent that night lodged in the fork of a tree, starting and holding her breath at every sound. She had no idea where she was—nor who or what might be pursuing her. Sleep was out of the question, and by dawn she was tired and miserable.

When it grew light she saw a thick clump of bushes not far off where she might lie and see without being seen. Accordingly, she slipped down and stole into her new cover, where she made as comfortable a nest as she could among the roots and fallen leaves.

She had not been there more than five minutes when she saw a strange party moving slowly through the orchard that stretched away below her. Four people wound slowly in and out of the trees. There were two soldiers with wicked looking lances, a thin priest and a boy. As they came nearer, Elena saw that the priest, who had his hood thrown back, was blind, and that the boy served as his eyes.

Haltingly they crossed a ditch at the edge of the orchard, and then seemed to wander aimlessly until they reached the tree where Elena had spent the night. To her horror, the blind man came to a halt, lifted his face as if testing the air and then pointed up into the tree. Instantly the soldiers sprang forward and, while one stood guard, the other clambered up the trunk.

The hair rose along the back of Elena's neck. Very, very gingerly she backed out of the bushes, never taking her eyes from her pursuers. When at last she was free, she turned and ran.

The rest of that day was like a nightmarish game of follow-the-leader. Sooner or later, no matter where she hid, or how she crossed and doubled her trail, she would find the little band drawing near, slowly, seemingly with no purpose, and she would have to run again, icy fear pulling at the pit of her stomach.

It soon became clear to her that the blind Priest was not following her trail, but was in some way drawn to *her*. Only his leisurely pace and the fact that he would stop wherever she had stopped while the soldiers investigated allowed her to elude the relentless search.

But Elena had other enemies as well: hunger and exhaustion. Thirst was no problem, for there were many fountains and pools in the Palace grounds. But her last meal was the one Ibby brought her when she was made a Lady. Nor had she slept since her night in the tower with the King.

Once, passing through the kitchen gardens, she stole what food she could and ate it on the run. The young carrots and radishes eased her hunger a little, and gave her a chance to think as she huddled near the stables, between a wall and a feed shed.

What a miserable business this is. What am I going to do? I'm getting so tired, but I don't dare sleep. If I do, I'll wake up on the end of a lance. Oh, I wish the Prince would come!

But it also occurred to her that the Prince might be waiting for word from *her*. It was quite likely that the Prince would continue to wait until it was too late. Too late for Elena, at least.

She thought wistfully of escape and freedom and the carefree days she had spent with Ariel, travelling from town to town.

At that, she took heart. *If I can just keep out of their way, sooner or later, someone's got to come.*

But her thoughts were cut short by the appearance in the distance of the searchers—the soldiers following doggedly, the boy, bored and indifferent, and the expressionless blind man, his attention turned inward towards some hidden sense, drawn on towards the magnet of Elena's being.

It was evening before it occurred to her that she might escape by the water. She had lost count of her flights from the terrible group, and had run along as many of the walls as she could. Convinced that there was no escape through or under or over them, she thought of the other boundary of her prison—the sea.

Making her way down towards the beach in the deepening dusk, she took shelter by a boathouse and surveyed the situation.

The Palace walls came down past the water's edge and extended some distance into the water. At either end was a beacon and a lookout's platform, manned by two archers. In the centre of the royal beach, a stout pier reached out from shore. Although several small boats were moored to it, Elena saw that there were two more archers on the pier, strolling up and down.

She sat in the shadows, wavering between hope and despair. *It's too far for me to swim. And if they saw me, I'd be a floating pincushion. I need a boat, but I'll have to wait until it's dark.*

With an uneasy glance over her shoulder, she settled down to watch and wait as long as she dared. But as she did, a man appeared bearing a torch. As the last light faded from the sky, the man lit the torches set along the length of the pier.

Without waiting for her pursuers, Elena made off through the darkness, choking down a sob of disappointment.

But with the night came relief, although Elena did not realize it at first. During the day she had become attuned to the rhythm of the chase, and had learned how much time she might expect before the detestable company came into sight. Now that they did not come, she became alarmed, thinking they must have circled round to approach from another side. But gradually the truth sank in: her hunters had stopped for the night.

Tears of relief rolled down her cheeks. She burrowed into a pile of dead leaves and instantly fell asleep.

When she woke again, the sky was lightening. Rising immediately, Elena went to a nearby pool for a drink, then risked a visit to the kitchen gardens for something to eat. She found very little, and despite the maddening aroma of baking bread, she did not dare approach the kitchens themselves.

And so began the deadly game's second day. She felt stronger for her sleep, but lack of food and the monotony of the chase began to tell on her. Several times she barely saved herself from being cornered, and once, in her flight, she almost blundered into a soldier, unaccountably standing guard outside a tea-house.

Flattening herself in the grass behind the little hut, Elena soon learned the reason for the soldier's presence. From inside the tea-house came voices. One she recognized as the King's. The other was too low to catch, but belonged, she was certain, to the High Priest, Chashra. They were arguing.

"No," she heard the King say. "I have given my word. Tomorrow will be soon enough." There was a low murmur, and the King replied with a bitter laugh. "A danger! What danger could there be, since you have taken everything from me? I would die today with a glad heart if I thought you had no entry to the Cities of the Dead!"

Elena stirred uneasily in the grass. Her time was growing short, and she was torn between her love for the King and her fear for the priest. She wanted to rush into the tea-house, but she did not dare. And then some movement in the distance caught her attention, and she was up and away, running silently to yet another hiding place, her heart grieving sorely for the King.

She had little time that day to consider the meaning of the fragment of conversation she had overheard. As the day wore on, the band of pursuers stepped up its pace, so that she was almost constantly on the move.

By the end of the day her hunger and the need for vigilance as she half walked, half ran from one refuge to another, made her shake with exhaustion.

They will catch me tomorrow, she thought dully, *if the Prince doesn't come*. She was hiding behind a statue of a bear, not far from the Palace. It was quiet and secluded, but she knew she had perhaps five minutes or so before she must run again to a new spot.

If he doesn't come, by tomorrow I just won't be able to run anymore, and they'll catch me, and that will be that. But I can still run now. She rolled over and sat up. *I think.*

And then, just as she was about to totter away again, a magnificent sound reached her ears. It was a peal of trumpets pouring out like liquid gold and fire from the Palace. Elena listened in wonder, tears starting to her eyes.

"He did it!" she whispered. "He came!"

27

Ropes and Fire

Staggering like a sailor home from the sea, giddy with relief, Elena lurched from her shelter and went at a faltering run to find the Prince. Her only clue was the trumpets which continued to shower peal upon peal upon her, and so she made for them. She went boldly now, for she did not care who saw her.

The sound seemed to come from one of the courtyards. As she went, kicking her weary legs along as though they were asleep, she passed some serving-folk, standing open-mouthed at the trumpets' call.

"The Prince has come!" she shouted to them as she went by. "The Prince has come!" But they did not seem to understand, and she staggered on alone.

She found the courtyard at last, a shadowy cleft in the vast stone bulk of the Palace. She flung herself through the wall of sound, and fell to her knees before the trumpeters.

Immediately, as though at a signal, the trumpets were silent. In a daze, Elena heard the last pure echoes die away, then a voice behind her spoke.

"Thus, O King, do all obey you. Whether they will or not."

With a convulsion of fear, Elena whirled about. Before her stood the King, but with Chashra, the Black Priest. There was no sign of Prince Yadral.

"Your Majesty—" she began.

"Bind her!" ordered the Priest.

Instantly she was seized, bound hand and foot, and dragged over to a post. When she was tied to this, the King stepped before her, and for a long moment stared into her face.

"It is sunset," he said at last. "Your three days are up." Elena saw that his eyes were red-rimmed, and that he looked once again shrunken and haggard. Like a ruined tower, she thought. Hovering just behind his shoulder, Chashra was the image of smug malevolence.

"He said the trumpets would bring you," the King muttered, and took a half step nearer to Elena. "Why did you come to the trumpets?"

Elena took a deep breath. "My lord, I—"

Chashra's voice slid like an eel between them. "O King, do not waste your thoughts upon this insolent witch, I pray you."

With a sudden flash of anger, the King spun around and gave the Priest a blow across the mouth. "Insolence!" he hissed. "I'll teach you insolence. Be silent when the King holds council!"

The mark of the blow stood out vividly on the Priest's pale face, and a thread of blood dribbled from his lower lip. He put out a pale tongue, dabbed delicately at the wound, then bowed without a word.

Turning again to Elena, the King said, "Why?"

"My lord King, I believed the trumpets announced the arrival of your son."

"You see he is not here."

"But he will come, my lord. I know it. I believe he waits for a message from me. If I were free—"

A mirthless smile crossed the King's face. "A message from you? Why would my son need a word from a common singing-girl?" In his face Elena saw royal pride tainted with the scorn of the Priests. "But you are not free," he went on. "You are condemned to fire with the rising of the sun. Do you wish to plead for your life?"

Elena felt tension in her chest, as though with every breath she lifted a great weight. "Not for my life, my lord. This was the King's decree. But I would beg you, my lord, not to abandon hope. Your son lives. He will come."

The King stared at her. It seemed to Elena that all around them was shadowy and unreal. In his eyes, she saw once more a desperate battle between hope and fear, but the spark of hope was a tiny one now. It was as though she looked down a long tunnel to see it.

Finally the King said, "You ask much of a man who has seen the mangled corpse of his son." He turned as if to go, hesitated, and then, in a voice thick with pain, added, "If he comes before the pyre is lit, you are free."

Chashra stood silent and unmoving until the King had left the courtyard. Then, with a gesture like a whip, he brought two soldiers forward. "Wood," he commanded. "Here."

It was dark. Alone in the courtyard, Elena stood tied to the post, surrounded by bundles of sticks piled chest high. High up in the walls of the Palace, one or two lights showed, but they only made the night seem darker and lonelier.

From time to time, Elena shifted her weight against the ropes, now resting her tired and aching legs, now easing the pressure across her chest. She had struggled, of course, but she knew there was no hope.

What is it like to die? she wondered, staring into the darkness. Once, on the road, Ariel told her about someone who had been ill for a long time. "And then," said Ariel, "one morning he just woke up and left." Elena had thought he meant "Woke up and got better," but she found out later that the man had died. "Then why did you say 'woke up'?" she demanded.

Ariel had laughed. "He was asleep. We all are. When he died, he woke up."

"Then, where was he when he woke up?"

But Ariel only laughed again and shrugged.

Now, I guess I'll find out, thought Elena. *I wish Ariel were here. Just to say good-bye.*

The bundles of wood were stacked so close to her that if she moved her leg, the sharp ends of sticks grazed her skin. She looked down and thought about the wood burning. *The flames will curl up, and I will only be able to jerk my leg away this much. But the fire will be all around me.*

To ease her mind, she lifted her eyes to the sky. By straining her neck she could glimpse a handful of stars against the black, and a sliver of the moon showing along the edge of the high Palace walls. The sight brought tears to her eyes.

I'll think of the moon. When they light the fire tomorrow, I'll think of the cool moon.

For the first time in her long ordeal, she gave way to her feelings. Huge sobs pushed up within her, tore open her heart and shook her against the post and ropes. She clenched her teeth and bit her lips to stifle any sound, but she could not stifle the sobs themselves, which racked through her like the thundering waves of the sea.

When at last the storm died away, she felt completely empty. No thought crossed her mind, nor any feeling her heart. She hung, slumped against the ropes, conscious only of the sweetness of the cool night air in her nostrils.

Much later, at dawn, the sound of steps on the flagstones of the courtyard roused her. Looking up with a sudden clutch of panic in her belly she saw a maid hurry across the far end of the courtyard with her head turned, but Elena knew that soon other steps would come, and with a far more serious intent.

She had not long to wait. Presently a company of soldiers marched in, led by their captain and the black figure of a Priest. Two of the soldiers carried torches. The soldiers formed two

134

lines before her, the two with torches nearest. The Priest raised a small iron bell and rang it once.

Gradually, several people appeared beyond the lines of soldiers. It was the King, with Chashra and two other priests. Then absolute silence prevailed. Time stood still. As suddenly as a clap of thunder, a ray of sunlight shot into the courtyard.

The King raised one hand.

"Now," said Chashra.

And the two torch-bearers stepped forward and lowered their brands to the dry wood.

28

Will Against Will

Elena shut her eyes, took a deep shuddering breath, and tried to picture the moon in her mind. Chaotic images rushed through instead. She saw the King, the Prince, the mill at Ballafan, Joan, the moon, the knot of Ismay. And Ariel saying, "Be above fear."

She felt hot. *Let it be quick. Please let it be quick.* She opened her eyes.

The scene before her was unchanged. Just across the piles of wood the soldiers still bent with their torches. Behind them stood the motionless lines, the Priests and the King. Beyond these, the delicate light of dawn fingered the granite blocks of the Palace. In the absolute stillness, Elena could hear the hissing of torch flames.

But the wood around her was not burning.

The torch-bearers shifted their torches, seeking a bundle that would light. They glanced uneasily at each other, muttered to themselves. One stole a quick glance at Elena, and then bent to his torch again. Seconds that seemed like hours dragged by.

Chashra's voice came cold and deadly: "Well? What is this delay? Kindle the pyre."

At this, one soldier thrust his torch so vigorously into the bundles that it extinguished. The other, after clearing his throat, said, "It—it won't light, sir."

"Fools," said Chashra, stepping forward, "you shall be next." He strode towards them, his hood thrown back, his eyes ablaze with anger. He lifted his hands and started to speak. But a few paces from the pyre, he stopped short. There was a moment of absolute stillness, and then he hissed angrily, "Who dares to challenge the black power?"

"I," said a voice. "I and all good men." And a figure stepped forward from among the soldiers. At the sight of him, it was all Elena could do not to shout with joy.

The Priest's face convulsed with hatred. "What are you?" he spat. "A common soldier! Nothing! I'll have you flogged!"

Ariel said, "Darkness shall not prevail. Renounce your hold upon the kingdom, and depart in peace."

The Priest stared coldly at Ariel. Finally he said, "So you have come at last. But you will do no good here. This is mine, do you understand? I have won!"

"Have you? said Ariel. "The sun still shines. The pyre remains unkindled. The King still rules."

But Chashra snapped, "Seize him. Bind him. He shall burn with her."

Two soldiers stepped forward, and then stopped, looking uncertainly from Ariel to the Priest. One looked to the King as well.

"Fools!" gritted Chashra. "Molak Gashag! Bind him!"

The soldiers began to move as though some unseen force compelled them. Jerkily they stepped forward, laid hold of Ariel and dragged him towards the pyre. Others stepped up like marionettes and drew their swords.

In a low voice Ariel said, "You are free. Be free."

The soldiers stopped, trembling.

"You are free," repeated Ariel, and those nearest him could not stand, and collapsed on the ground, while the others stood frozen.

"You too are free," said Ariel to the Priest, "or can be, if you choose."

"I will be free of *you*," said Chashra, and drew from under his robes a dagger fashioned like a snake.

At that moment Elena saw the world go dark. Only Ariel and Chashra with his gleaming dagger stood in light, as though performing a bright and deadly dance.

But Ariel was unarmed. Elena could not understand where his soldier's weapons had gone. But weaponless he stood before the Priest, who advanced, dagger ready.

Slowly they circled, stepping lightly as cats. Then, without warning, Chashra's arm flicked out towards Ariel's face. But Ariel was not there. In that same instant he had ducked and dodged to safety.

Chashra whirled and was on him again. Just as quickly, Ariel dodged. Again and again Chashra struck in a furious rage. Each time Ariel just barely escaped the vicious bite of the knife. Finally, one thrust hit its mark and opened a red line along Ariel's cheek.

Chashra paused and allowed himself a cruel smile.

"You are doomed," he said. "There is poison. You would do better to take a quick death from the knife. Will you?"

Before Ariel could reply, the Priest leapt forward. Even as he did Ariel twisted aside and kicked upwards, catching the Priest's wrist with his toe.

Chashra gave a shriek of pain and the knife went spinning into the air. Then it came down, point first on the stones and the blade shattered.

The two men stood staring at each other, breathing heavily. Then the Priest raised both his hands and began to speak.

"Ash-malak, smaoxas ksast samaogh . . ."

The ring of light shrank ever smaller as he spoke. Ariel stood immobile while the harsh words of power and darkness rolled on. Elena felt all life leaving her, and she thought, *It's over. We're dying. We did our best, and failed.*

Chashra finished his chant. With a mighty yell, he cast the spell at Ariel.

Ariel simply raised one hand and spoke one word, so that the spell turned back and fell with all its force upon the Priest.

There was a flash, a whizzing snap like an enormous whip, and an acrid stinging in the nostrils. When Elena could see clearly again, the Priest was gone. All that remained was a smouldering pile of black robes.

And the darkness had vanished. In normal light, she could see the soldiers blinking and beginning to stir.

She also saw the three other Priests. Stunted by evil and fear, they crouched in the daylight and seemed more pitiful than frightening. But they had drawn daggers and laid hold of the King. Now they were edging away, intent on using him to obtain their safe passage.

Seeing this, one of the soldiers drew his sword and leapt upon them with a yell. He grasped the King and hurled him aside to safety, and then with mighty strokes hewed down two of the Priests where they stood. The third Priest fled shrieking, but did not go ten paces before the same soldier felled him with one blow.

"Quick, men," he shouted to the other soldiers. "Up and cleanse the Palace!"

Elena was not surprised to find herself in tears. The soldier was Prince Yadral, come home at last.

Ariel, at the King's bidding, released Elena from her captivity.

"Ariel," she said anxiously, as he undid the ropes, "your face . . . the poison . . ."

He smiled. "Never mind, dear heart. It was a lie."

He caught her as she fell, and carried her into the Palace.

29

Words of Praise and Farewell

Light streamed into the great Audience Hall, illuminating the ceremonial banners and bright costumes of the people who thronged the floor. On the dais, whole again but tired, sat the King. Beside him sat Prince Yadral.

Three days had passed since what the Prince now called the Day of Liberation; three days of intense activity, of restoration and reconciliation. Now the King had opened the Audience Hall for the first time in long months and invited in the citizens of Estria.

Elena was there, standing with Ariel, near one end of the dais. Down the hall, Elena could see Lord and Lady Fabiad, looking as though nothing unusual had happened in the last hundred years. On the other side of the dais, ready to serve, stood Ibby, now the King's personal steward. And beyond Ibby, leaning heavily on a stick, stood the gaunt figure of Barkat. Still pale and weak from his imprisonment, his shining eyes seemed in love with all they saw.

At a signal, heralds at the four corners of the hall raised their trumpets and sounded a mighty peal. As the echoes died away, all stood silent, awaiting the pleasure of the King. He sat for a long moment observing them. Then he spoke.

"Beloved Children of Estria, faithful servants, peace and welcome to you all. It has been too long since I have met you here, but I will speak briefly.

"It is no secret I have been away. Not in body, but in heart and mind I have been absent from the court for months. I have neglected the duties of a ruler. I have followed counsel most unwise, and in every way I have served you badly. Indeed, it is only through the heroic efforts of some faithful ones among you that the Kingdom was saved from destruction.

"There can be no excuse for such a breach of trust, nor can I hope for your forgiveness. I propose therefore, with your approval, to abdicate the throne of Estria in favour of my son, Prince Yadral, Appin bar talib."

An astonished and uneasy silence followed the King's words. The people had gathered in relief and anticipation, hoping for a return to the life they had known before. Now they teetered once again upon the brink of the unknown.

"Your Majesty! With your permission," said Lord Fabiad, and bowed. "The House of Fabiad stands loyal to the throne of Estria and bears deep love for both your Majesty and your son. We expect that in the natural passage of time Prince Yadral will ascend the throne, and no doubt prove himself an apt and even-handed ruler. But your Majesty has earned the wisdom of experience, a wisdom we need sorely now, for there is much to do. We humbly beg therefore, my lord, that you remain our king."

Heads nodded at this. One by one, others stood forth to say the same or similar: They loved the King, they wanted him to stay.

At last, when many had spoken, and not one had supported abdication, the King raised his hand. "Beloved subjects, I am unworthy, but I hear your wish and I obey. I—" But here his speech was swallowed by a tremendous cheering. When at last it quietened, and the King could speak again, his cheeks were wet with tears.

"I thank you," he said humbly. "I will try to be worthy of your trust.

"Dear ones, I invite you all to a feast this night. I had thought it would be to honour a new king, but in truth, I think it should be to honour those who brought us through the darkness."

He paused and looked about the hall. "There were many who preserved the flame. My son. Lord and Lady Fabiad. Lord Orrime. Many others. Their stories will be sung and told tonight. But I myself owe the most perhaps to—" He sought her out and beckoned. "Elena, come here."

Blushing furiously, Elena approached the throne, eyes downcast.

"The faith and heart and truthfulness of this girl preserved me in my darkest hour," the King said. "I commend her to you. Whatever you may do for her will be a favour done to me."

This time Prince Yadral led the cheering. Never in her life had Elena heard anything so loud.

The banquet had reached its third hour and was dissolving into a blur of songs, toasts and speeches, when Ariel sought out Elena and drew her aside.

"Well?" he said, and she understood, instantly.

"All right," she said. "But I have no pack, and no clothes either."

"I have them," he said. "But first we must find the Prince. Come."

Prince Yadral was in a quiet alcove, deep in conversation with Barkat. At their appearance, he stood and clasped their hands.

"Ariel, Elena," he said, "you are the heroes of the feast."

"There are others who deserve it more, perhaps," said Ariel. "But the feast will go on without us. We have come to take our leave."

"No, Ariel," said the Prince. "Can we not persuade you

to stay? We owe you both so much. We would gladly treat you and fete you for a year.''

Ariel grinned. ''The more reason to go,'' he said. ''We would forget how to work for a living. We will come back, I promise you, but with my lord's permission, we will leave tonight.''

''So be it,'' sighed the Prince, ''though it grieves my heart to part with you. Elena, my father gave you leave of the Palace, and for the love you bear him and your valiant heart, you are always welcome here. Ariel, if I thought you would take it, I would offer you whatever I have.''

Ariel smiled, a flash of white teeth in his thin brown face. ''We are brothers,'' he said. ''That is more than I could wish for.''

Barkat had been watching all with his luminous, peaceful gaze, but especially Elena. When they embraced to say farewell, he held her gently for a moment and whispered, ''Adab, little sister. Adab.'' And then the moment was gone, and she and Ariel were slipping away to a quiet room where their packs and travelling gear awaited them.

It was a strange old-new sensation Elena felt as she stepped out of her court clothes and into her familiar travelling ones. So much had happened since she wore them last—was it only a week ago?

''He said something to me,'' she told Ariel as she changed. ''Barkat, that is.''

''What did he say?''

''It sounded like 'adab.' ''

Ariel chuckled. ''I should have known he would.''

''What?''

''He gave you an initiation, a high one in the Brotherhood. It's all right. It's a blessing, though you may not always think so.''

Elena stood nonplussed. Then she shrugged. "I still don't know what it means."

"You will someday. Are you ready?"

"Yes."

"Come, then." And they shouldered their packs and stole quietly from the palace.

But when they stepped out into the cool night air, two figures barred their way.

"You see," said one. "I told you."

"Without even saying good-bye!" said the other.

It was Lou and Joan.

"Dear hearts," said Ariel. "We must. But we'll come back."

"I know," said Joan. "We only wanted to say good-bye." And they embraced one another.

"When you come back," Joan said to Elena, "we'll spend whole days together." But Lou said nothing, only squeezed her hard and kissed her. Then they melted away into the night.

In the darkness, Ariel reached out and took Elena's hand. "It's a fine night for travelling," he said.

"Where shall we go?"

He laughed. "Well, I don't know, but I feel the urge to try the life of a miller for a time. Let's be off to Ballafan."

And so they set out through the streets of Rakhbad, favoured by the light of a rising moon.